TWISTED
reality

TWISTED
reality

HEIDI MCLAUGHLIN

COVER DESIGN: Sarah Hansen at Okay Creations.
EDITING: There For You Editing
COPYEDITING: Virginia Carey
INTERIOR DESIGN: Tianne Samson with

E.M.
TIPPETTS
BOOK DESIGNS

emtippettsbookdesigns.com

CHAPTER
one

Joey

"Joey, I know we're already married, but I would really like to do things right. Will you marry me in front of our family and friends? Will you be my partner in all things and marry me … again?"

My teeth press together in both a form of anger and excitement. *This* is what I wanted weeks ago, the declaration and commitment, and now that I'm getting it, I don't know what to do. Everyone in the audience is yelling at me to say yes, or they're saying they'll marry him. I want to remind them all that he comes with an incredible amount of baggage in the name of Jules Maxwell and that may be too much for most people to handle.

The host, Helen, is looking at me, anxiously waiting for my answer. In fact, everyone is staring at me, and suddenly I'm too hot and sweat is starting to run down my face, ruining my make-up. Over Josh's shoulder, there's a producer holding his hand up, like he's asking me to stop or stall my answer.

Josh laughs and I wonder if he finds this comical or if he's placating the audience because I'm taking too long. Is there a set time limit on when you have to answer a marriage proposal? I'm trying to decide my future here, and up until a minute ago, I thought I was headed for divorce court.

Josh and I make eye contact and that's when I see it, the sincerity in his proposal. My eyes fall to the black velvet box he's holding, where the cushioned diamond ring catches the studio lights overhead, sparkling brightly as a result. I remember his words from the beginning about my ring and know that he's doing this the right way. Finally, my eyes land on the producer with his hand still up in the air and I realize I don't care about this show, or anyone's ratings, I only care about Josh.

"Yes," I reply, covering my mouth to avoid crying out with happiness. "Yes, Josh, I'll marry you."

He stands, pulls me into his arms, and swings me around before kissing me in front of the live studio audience. "I love you, Joey," he says in between kisses and I tell him that I love him, too. My love for him is beyond the crazy stalker fan kind of love. It's genuine and heartfelt. He makes me happy. He makes me laugh. Most importantly, he makes me want to be a better person.

As soon as he sets me down, he slips the ring on my finger where it fits perfectly. Our friends congratulate us and the make-up assistant rushes out to once again fix our faces. When I glance at Josh, he's wiping tears that have fallen from his eyes. My heart beats faster knowing that our future has moved him in such a way that he's cried. The make-up staff tells me I'm done, so I sit back down and can feel someone staring at me. I know it's Bronx and I know he doesn't approve, but this isn't his life, it's mine. I purposely avoid looking over at him because I don't need to see the expression on his face. He has his happiness and he should be happy for me, no matter who I choose to be with.

"Welcome back," Helen says as she faces the camera. Josh puts his arm around me and instead of him pulling me close I go willingly. "When we left you, Josh was on bended knee asking Joey to marry him." Helen looks at us and I can't hide the smile on my face. I flash my hand and the audience cheers again, which is likely on cue, but I don't care. I'm engaged to remarry the man that I love.

"So when's the big day?" Helen asks.

"Well, we're already married so I think we can take some time to plan whatever type of wedding Joey wants."

"Josh is due to start filming his new movie starting next week, so sometime after that," I add, smiling at him. He leans forward and kisses my nose, earning a resounding ahh from the crowd. I'm giddy. I can't help it. He makes me feel like a fairytale princess, showing me that dreams do come true.

"Millie and Cole, do you have anything you'd like to share with us?"

We all turn our attention to them and wait. Bronx and Rebekah are here as well. Gary and Amanda are getting a divorce and opted not to travel with us.

Cole looks at Millie and forces a smile. There is something going on between them, but I don't know what it could be. She doesn't seem as happy as she was when we were in the house. Smiling softly, Millie meets Helen's gaze. "We're pregnant!" Her voice is an octave higher, but it doesn't carry the usual enthusiasm an expectant mother would normally carry.

Once again, the audience cheers for them and the rest of us clap our hands and offer them our congratulations. Josh presses his lips to my ear, causing me to hold my breath. Is he going to tell me he wants to have a baby, too? It'd be silly to think that considering how much animosity he has toward his parents. It's going to be a long time before he's ready to have children, if he ever is.

The attention is now on Rebekah and Bronx, but they

have nothing to report, other than being happily married and thankful that they didn't have to spend the full ninety days on the show. I'm still pissed about that. They only participated in a handful of competitions and were still eligible for the grand prize. I was really hoping Rebekah would be asked about her relationship with Gary, but Helen is far too classy for something like that.

Once we have another commercial break, we're excused. Backstage, Millie grabs my arms and jumps up and down. This is like when that really cute boy you've been crushing on asks you to prom and you have to run to the bathroom with your bestie to celebrate, except everyone is watching us.

"I'm so happy for you," Millie exclaims.

"Me? What about you? You're going to have a baby, so no more jumping up and down! You'll give your baby a headache."

Her face falls when I bring up the baby. For someone who is happily married she doesn't seem too happy to be pregnant.

"What's wrong?"

Millie subtly shakes her head and looks for Cole. I look as well and find him in deep conversation with Josh. I motion for Millie to move over to the corner so we can have a little privacy. I make sure her back is facing Cole so he can't see that we're talking about him.

"Why are you so sad?" My hands rub up and down her arms while she wipes away her tears.

"Cole's mother doesn't like me."

"That's not uncommon. It's hard for a mother to give up her son."

"No, you don't understand," she says as she wipes her nose. "When he took me over to meet her the other day, she had a lawyer sitting in the living room with divorce papers. Cole told her that we're pregnant and she said I did it to trap him. How can I trap him on a show where we were legally married?"

"Oh, honey, I don't know. Maybe she's just overprotective or something." I honestly don't know what to say to Millie. I can't imagine being in her shoes right now. They fell in love on the show and their baby is living proof. I was often jealous of them, wanting what they were sharing to happen with Joshua. How can I offer advice when I don't know what to tell her? Take your husband, your money, and run? Would Cole go with her? Would he still choose her?

"What does Cole have to say?" I ask, needing to know if he's a momma's boy or if he's going to stand up for his wife and unborn child.

"That's just it, he won't talk about it. Every time I try to bring it up, he changes the subject or kisses me senseless, hoping I'll forget. But I can't forget, Joey. She *hates* me."

"Maybe she needs to get to know you?"

Shaking her head, Millie wipes her tears again. Her make-up is smudged, her eyes bloodshot and red-rimmed. I feel bad, angry even. Cole's mother could at least try to get to know her daughter-in-law. Although I say this as if it should be easy, I'm not looking forward to meeting Josh's parents. Mine are another story; they're already excited to meet him. Probably more excited that they have a son now and no longer need me.

"I offered, ya know, to go out to lunch after we were done with this tour and she just looked at me like I have two heads. Then she ranted about the money and the house that's ours if we stay married a year—she told Cole he won't need it."

Millie slumps against the wall, clearly defeated and overwhelmed. I pat her back, which is probably annoying the crap out of her, but I don't know what else to do. Looking over her shoulder, I catch Josh eyeing me. His eyes sort of bug out in that 'what the hell is going on over there' look and points to his watch. I shrug and he discretely motions toward Cole. Great! We've become the Brooks' marriage counselors despite the fact that we have our own issues.

I may have said yes to his proposal, but that doesn't mean I've forgotten about the crap with Jules. Something tells me that by the end of the night I'll be shedding my own tears over her, Josh, and this whole situation. I love him though, and I made the mistake of letting my heart control my emotions. He broke down my walls piece by piece, inserting his presence into my life even though he tried to fight it. Before I knew it I was no longer a fan with a crush, I was a woman in love with a man who just so happens to be a movie star.

Coming over to me, Josh whispers into my ear, "We should think about going." Between the feel of his hand on my back and his voice in my ear, I'm a wobbly-kneed schoolgirl who is willing to follow him anywhere. He kisses me softly before moving away, giving me some privacy to say good-bye to Millie.

"I know, you need to go," she says, offering me a soft smile. I pull her into a hug.

"We'll see each other soon. Josh and I have some things to work out, like living arrangements, and once we do we'll have you and Cole come out for a nice long weekend or something."

"Okay," she says, nodding.

I take her hands in mine and make sure she's looking at me. "Millie, I promise we're going to see each other and I want to be at your baby shower. I'm only a phone call away, okay?"

"Okay," she answers timidly.

I hug her again. "Call me before you leave Los Angeles and we'll meet up."

She nods and tells me good-bye. I'm hesitant to leave her and when I look back, Cole is standing there next to her. I can only hope that he doesn't care what his mother thinks and he'll fight to keep Millie happy. As soon as I come around the corner, Josh is in a heated conversation with a man I've never seen before. I stop, staying back in case he's discussing business. I don't want him to think that I have to know everything, but I do hope that he shares.

He spots me and smiles as he reaches for me. The second our hands connect I feel like I can breathe again.

"Joey, this is Barry, one of the producers from the show."

I shake his hand and immediately mold into Josh's side.

"It's nice to meet you, Joey. As I was telling Josh, we'd like to broadcast your life."

"What do you mean?" I ask with a bit of confusion.

"They want to make a reality show about us, follow us around. That sort of thing," Josh answers. The thought of having cameras follow me around again does not excite me at all. I didn't even want to go on the show to begin with, and I really don't want to share my life with anyone other than Josh and our families.

"Um …" I say, hesitating. I look to Josh for an answer.

"We'll get back to you, Barry. Joey and I need to talk about it first."

"We'll make it worth your while. Here's our proposal." Barry hands Josh some folded papers, which he quickly places in his pocket. He pulls me behind him in a rush until we're outside and being ushered into a black town car. Once the door shuts, his lips are on mine with his fingers tangling in my hair.

"I've missed you," he says over and over again in between kisses.

CHAPTER
two

Joshua

I've waited for this moment since the season finale of *Married Blind*. This is how Joey and I should've been right after the show—in our personal car, heading to the hotel and in each other's arms—but instead she was with Bronx and I was left chasing after her.

It's taken me weeks to find her and it's not like she was missing. She was there, just out of my reach. But now I have her and she's agreed to spend the rest of her life with me. Asking her to marry me, even though we're technically already married, in front of the live audience was risky. My proposal could've backfired and honestly, I half expected it to. There could've been a slap across the face, which I likely deserve. She could've said no and I would deserve that as well, but I wouldn't have given up. Not on her. Not on us.

As much as I fought falling for her, I was doomed from the moment I kissed Joey on stage right at the start of the show. I had never felt that way before. My body was zinging, everything was in hyper-color and I felt so alive. It's cheesy to say she was made for me, but there isn't any other way to explain the connection I feel with her. Walking away at the end of the season was never going to be an option for me, and no matter how many times I told her we were just friends in the house, I knew deep down I was lying to myself.

Joey nestles into the crook of my neck. Just holding her like this is worth the pain and suffering I've been through during the past few weeks. The agony of not knowing how she really felt was killing me slowly. I adjust slightly, trying to bring her even closer and kiss the top of her head, letting my lips linger there.

I don't know how to be a husband. I suppose most men say this at some time in their lives, but the difference is they most likely had a solid upbringing whereas I had utter shit. My father is not the type of man I want to be … however; Hollywood predicts that's exactly how I'll end up. Like father like son, right? Aside from a few celebrities, marriages do not last here. The time away from each other, the constant rumors, and the never-ending temptation, are a surefire way to destroy your life, your marriage.

"I'm going to be strong for you," I absentmindedly say out loud. Joey pulls her head away from my shoulder and looks at me, her forehead furrowed in confusion. I shouldn't have opened my mouth and now it's too late.

"What are you talking about?"

I quickly avert my gaze out the car window and see that we're a block or so from the hotel. Glancing at the driver, I frown—not at him, but at the situation I've now created for myself.

"We're almost at the hotel," I murmur, pushing her hair behind her ear. It's crazy to think that her hair has gotten longer since I've last seen her, but I swear it has. Right now, my wife doesn't look like the one I fell in love with. Joey, inside the house, never wore make-up and her hair was always in a ponytail or in a bun. I look at her now, and while she's still gorgeous, I don't like seeing all that crap painted on her face. I hate that I can't run my fingers through her hair because the spray holding the curls in place prevents me from doing so.

The second the driver pulls up to the curb, light bulbs flash and the continuous clicking of cameras start. I take her hand in mine and ask if she's ready. This is our first public appearance, outside of television, and the press is going to be all over her.

"Whatever you do, don't let go of my hand. Okay?"

"Okay," she says, nodding, squeezing my hand for good measure.

I take a deep breath as the driver appears on the passenger side of the car, along with hotel security. As he opens the door, the noise grows louder. Our names are called, questions are hurled, and when Jules' name is mentioned I try to walk a bit faster to get inside the sanctity of the hotel. I think about hanging my head, but I don't. I stand proud and let them take my picture, because right now I feel like I can conquer the world with my wife by my side.

My wife.

Just thinking those words brings me a sense of calm. My life feels like it's finally heading in the right direction and it's all because of Joey and her willingness to take the risk of being in my life. If I were Joey, I'd run for the hills and not look back. I'm not worthy of her love, but I'm going to do every damn thing I can to prove that I deserve it.

When we finally reach our room, I pick her up—much to her delight—and set my hand with the keycard against the magnetic lock to open the door. I anticipated her saying yes, or at least coming back here with me, so I had the room prepared.

Rose petals are scattered around the floor, and a bottle of champagne together with strawberries and a small wedding cake sit on a small table to the side. The bedroom should be more of the same with an array of lingerie waiting for her in case she wants to wear something like that to bed. I didn't want to be presumptuous, but she did wear those types of things while on the show, although I'd be happy if she just wore my shirt.

"This moment should've happened the day we left the show," I say before putting her down.

"It's beautiful, Josh." She doesn't leave my side like I expected her to. Instead, she keeps her arm around my waist and leaves us both standing in the room wondering what's next.

We need to talk. We need to get shit out in the open— especially about what happened after the show was over. I can't have anything that Jason did hanging over our heads.

"Is that cake?" she asks, breaking the silence.

"Yeah. I thought we could … well, not smear it all over each other's faces, but enjoy a slice or two. It's probably not as good as yours, though."

Joey glances at me, smiling. "You're rambling."

"I'm nervous," I say, shrugging.

"Don't be." Joey walks over to the cake and swipes a bit of frosting off the side. "Yum." She licks it off her finger, humming her satisfaction. She walks over to the window with her finger still in her mouth, which sends a nice jolt straight to my groin.

When she reaches for the handle of the sliding glass door I cringe. "The cameras are out there."

Joey turns and winks. "We can pretend we're the Royals and step out onto the balcony and kiss for them."

"Is that something you want to see? You're going to be all over the tabloids."

"It's part of your life, right?" she asks.

"It is, but you can ignore them."

She beckons me with her finger and I move toward her willingly. "If I'm going to be your wife I need to accept all

11

of you, including your professional life. For three months I didn't have to share you with the world." She sort of nods and shakes her head at the same time after she says that. "I know what I'm getting into, Josh. I happen to think that if we're more willing to appease them, they'll leave us alone when we want our privacy."

Maybe she has a point. I don't really know because the press has only ever hounded me about my life.

"If you think it's best." Reaching for her hand, I guide us out onto the balcony. We both lean over at the same time and do a little people watching until someone yells our names. Once that happens, they scurry to get into position to take our photos.

"They're crazy."

"You have no idea," I tell her. "But it's their job. They have families to feed."

"But they're aggressive!" Joey peers over the balcony, enticing the crowd below to get louder. Unfortunately, our suite is somewhat low to the ground so the photographers are getting decent shots.

"Some are, others respect you. It's when they're crawling through your bushes that you start having issues with them."

Joey blanches and I shrug. I'm used to it.

"Come stand next to me," she says, hooking her arm with mine. I lean down and kiss her and the media frenzy below us erupts. She smiles against my lips, hopefully because I'm kissing her and not at what is happening on the streets. She's going to quickly realize that being followed and having your every move captured is intrusive and very annoying.

"I think we should go inside," I whisper into her ear, another perfect shot for the cameras. She nods against me, slipping her hand into mine and following me back into our room where I shut and lock the door and pull the privacy curtains closed. The last thing I need is for any part of her body to be spread across the papers in the morning.

Joey is moving around the room, side-stepping the rose petals on the floor as if it's some type of game. I watch, in awe of her beauty, as she giggles and tries to balance herself so she doesn't fall over.

"What are you looking at?" she asks as she tips her head shyly.

"My wife," I answer with an inflection in my voice.

There's a visible change in her demeanor when those words register with her. I walk toward her, careful not to mess up the petals on the floor in case she wants to dance around them again, and lift her chin to meet my gaze.

"My wife," I say again, and watch her eyes flutter and her cheeks turn rosy. "My wife." This time the words are a mere whisper as I repeat myself, if not for me, but for her so she knows that I'm right where I want to be.

"I love you, Joey. And I'm sorry for what happened after the show, but know this: I never had any intention of letting you go—I don't care what I said in the house. From the moment I kissed you on stage, I knew you were going to be in my life and I fought my attraction to you until I couldn't anymore."

"I think you already know how I feel."

"I do," I tell her. "Most people in my position would freak out being married to a fan, but you're the only person that sees the real me and if that hasn't scared you away, I don't know what will."

Sighing, Joey steps into my arms. Her head rests against my shoulder and her fingers grip the back of my shirt, almost as if she's trying to keep me here.

"Jules scares me," she says, mumbling into my chest.

I pull her tighter to me and kiss the top of her head before leading her over to the couch. When she sits, I reach for her legs and bring them onto my lap so I can get as close to her as possible and still be able look into her eyes.

"I'm not going to sugar coat any of this, Joey, so if you

have any questions, you ask and I'll answer them honestly. I have no secrets."

"Okay."

Shit, I was hoping she'd start with a question. Inhaling deeply, I steady myself for what could be an ugly conversation.

"There was a time when I thought I'd be with Jules forever. She wanted marriage and I didn't. In fact, until I married you the thought had never crossed my mind. For a while we were serious, but it wasn't enough for her and she became emotionally comfortable with Bronx. Jules says she didn't cheat, but I'm not confident in her truth telling so we broke up and did this whole off and on thing for a bit. Jules, for the most part, was a casual hook-up because I felt she was safe."

"Have you been with her since the show?"

My eyes narrow in on Joey, hating that she even felt she needed to ask this of me. "No, hell fucking no. She was there when the show was over, and I told her to get lost. In fact, she's supposed to star opposite me in that movie I am slated to start filming, but I told my agent no way in hell am I working with her and to have the director find someone else or I'm out."

Joey tries to shift away from me, but I don't want her to leave me. Instead, I bring her onto my lap and move us to the corner of the sofa for more comfort. "Believe me when I tell you that she's not who I want. I don't really care if I never see her again."

"She'll be back, Josh. Scorned women rarely take no for an answer."

"If she comes back, she'll see how happily married and in love I am, and realize that she'll never have a place in my heart. It's all yours, Joey, there's no room for anyone else."

We sit like this, in silence, holding each other for longer than I thought we would. In my mind, I figured we'd be shedding our clothes and truly consummating our marriage.

14

I don't blame her really for wanting to wait. I suppose if the tables were turned I'd feel the same way.

She tries to get up. "I need to take a shower."

"Can I come with you?" I ask, waggling my eyes at her. She laughs and nods, bringing me a little more comfort.

"California is always in a drought, right? We might as well conserve water."

"Yes, we should." I walk behind her with my hands on her hips as I try to kiss her neck. "We need to talk about living arrangements, too. My apartment is small and I have a roommate. Plus, I'll be leaving soon."

"Do you want me to stay in L.A.?" she asks as she turns in my arms. The thought hadn't occurred to me that she could go home while I was filming. The only problem with that is the media will eat her alive, assuming we've split up again, and I don't want her to have that kind of drama.

"No, I think tomorrow we'll look for a place together."

"What about your roommate?"

"I'll help him find someone to take my spot."

Joey turns again and pulls her hair to the side. She peers over her shoulder with a wicked glint in her eye.

"Can you help me?"

"With pleasure, Mrs. Wilson."

"Ooh, I like the sound of that."

"Mhm, I like the sound your zipper makes as it reveals your back to me." I'm instantly hard, just by staring at her back.

She pulls the front off and lets the dress pool at her feet. My wife is rocking a white thong with a garter that I find incredibly sexy. When she faces me, her breasts are bare and my erection is playing tentmaker behind my trousers.

"You're wearing too many clothes," she says, pointing her finger.

My clothes start to come off quicker than I can count to five. Joey methodically removes the garters, one clip at time, teasing me with every flick of her finger, and begins rolling her stockings down her legs. As soon as my drawers are around my ankles, she shimmies out of her thong, letting it fall to join the rest of her clothes.

"Before we get into the shower, I have something to say."

"What's that, Joey?"

She steps closer to me, her taut nipples pressing against my chest. "You have a lot of making up to do and it starts now."

Before I can respond, she steps into the shower and turns on the water. "Well fuck me, my wife has a dirty side."

CHAPTER
three

Joey

"What did you mean when you said you'll be strong for me in the car?" My fingers play with Josh's chest, roaming over the planes of his abs and pecs. His abs are like a maze, except I can't solve it. Every now and again, he stills my hand because I'm tickling him, only to let it go so I can start over again.

"I think I spoke without thinking," he replies. "But now that I think about it, it means I'm going to be taking the brunt of everything coming our way."

"What does that mean?" Sitting up on my elbow, I look at him quizzically. The white sheet falls away, exposing my breasts. Josh takes his finger and runs it down over my breast, making me shiver.

"Drama," he says, sighing. "I have a feeling that Jules isn't going to go away any time soon, and I don't want you to worry about her. I don't love her, never did. You're the one I'm in love with and I can't imagine not telling you that every day, multiple times a day."

Josh pulls me close, capturing my lips. Every kiss since I said yes has been different. Instead of butterflies taking flight, leaving me tingling, it's fireworks on New Year's Eve or the most thrilling rollercoaster at Disney. It's the hairs on my arms standing on end, and goose bumps prickling my skin. It's like he was reserved during our stint on reality TV and now that we're together and the cameras are off, he's being himself. The *real* Joshua Wilson and not the celebrity who I'm used to holding back on his feelings while in public. It's still hard to think he was acting inside the house because I know he wasn't, but that's the only way I can explain it.

"She doesn't scare me," I tell him with a bite of authority, even though I don't believe those words at all. She scares the shit out of me. I know I'm supposed to keep my enemies close and all that crap, but I don't want her anywhere near me. In fact, if Josh and I could go live on a deserted island I'd be content. That would mean I'd be able to keep him all to myself.

"I won't let her anywhere near you," he says, reassuring me that I won't have to deal with her. I'm not stupid, though. They run in the same social circles, attending the same parties and galas. Unless he's intending on keeping me home, I'll see her, and when she's eyeing my husband I'll be sure to flash my ring so she sees it every single time. It's me who wears his ring, not her.

I know I sound petty and vindictive. I can't help it. Right now I'm living this fairytale romance—one I never thought I'd have—and it would be foolish to think our lives are going to be perfect.

"Are you hungry?" he asks, nipping at my neck.

"A little."

"For what?" Now he's moved to my breast, pulling one of my nipples between his teeth.

"Well I know what you're hungry for."

"Always, my wife. All the fucking time; I want to be

buried to the hilt inside of your pussy." His words eat up my flesh, causing me to blush.

"I love how easily I can turn you on," he says, sliding a finger between my folds. My eyes roll back in my head as I try to focus on him. "We are going to have an amazing sex life."

"Is that so?"

Josh pushes the rest of the sheet off of us, exposing his hard on. He strokes it a few times and even as I watch him, I can feel his eyes roaming all over my body. I lick my lips in anticipation of what's to come. A shiver goes through me as I picture myself sitting on top of him with my head thrown back in ecstasy. Sex with him is the one fantasy that he hasn't left me disappointed. I had always imagined what it would be like with Josh and he's delivered each and every time.

I straddle his lap and grab his shaft to guide him into my wet center. Slowly, I ease myself down onto him while his hands remain steady on my hips. My fingers dig into his abdomen as he closes his eyes and pushes his head back into his pillow.

"Don't move yet," he murmurs, meeting my gaze.

"Why not?" When I shimmy my hips, his hands clamp down, adding pressure to my hipbone.

"I just want this moment, so I can memorize you like this."

"Like what?"

"The way you look right now with my dick buried deep inside of you with your pink flesh and your nipples peaked ready for my mouth."

"Joshua Wilson, I never knew you were so damn dirty." I rock my hips forward as his grip tightens.

"I never knew sex could be so empowering. You're like the charge of electricity that I need to fucking live. I've never felt this way before."

With his words I push his hands above his head and

leave them there. I'm not strong enough to hold him down so I can only hope he complies with my silent request. Rising up to plant my feet on the bed and placing my hands on his stomach for leverage, I push myself off his erection, only to slide back down again.

"Fuck me." He watches his dick move in and out of me. "This is the hottest thing I have ever seen."

Even though I suspect otherwise, I'm choosing to believe him. I'm choosing to listen to everything he says when he tells me that he's never felt like this.

My legs tire quickly, forcing me to change positions. I rock toward him, letting my breasts drag against his chest.

"Touch me," I beg, needing to feel him.

"Fuck yes." Sitting up, he immediately takes one breast in his mouth. He alternates between sucking and biting while his other hand disappears between us and his finger starts rubbing and pinching my clit.

"You're so deep." The words that tumble out of my mouth in a non-coherent sentence seem to spur him on because he shifts positions, pulls me down to his chest, and starts thrusting into me. I scream out as my orgasm rushes through my body, making me convulse with pleasure.

Josh grunts as his release finds him and his limbs go weak. We're both still, too tired to move and unwilling to disengage from each other.

"I've just decided you can't stay here or move back home while I'm filming."

I laugh, causing his still somewhat erect penis to flex inside of me.

"Do that again, babe."

I do this repeatedly until he starts moving slowly inside of me. The slow ministrations are welcomed and before I know it I'm flat on my back with my legs over his shoulders. Our releases are quick this time and feel more like aftershocks. It's like we needed this extra bit to finish us both off.

He rolls off of me, pulling me into his side. "So like I was saying …"

"Yes, about me not staying here."

"Yeah, you're definitely coming to Alabama with me because there's no way in hell I'm going to survive without being inside of you for that long."

"You can survive without sex, Josh."

Josh pops up onto his side, startling me. "Woman, do not make me hog-tie you and drag your ass to Alabama."

"I've never been tied up," I interject. He drops his head and groans, before looking at me again.

"Seriously, though, Joey. I don't want us to be apart from each other. After a long day at work I want to come back to your arms and make love to you. We'll rent a suite at a hotel, and while I'm working you can explore or take some of the local tours. When I'm not working, we'll walk hand-in-hand while we sightsee and have a mini-honeymoon."

"That's what I wanted, too, Josh."

"Then why didn't you tell me?" he asks, cupping my cheek.

"I was afraid."

He doesn't ask of what because I'm sure he knows. Leaning forward, he kisses me softly, letting his lips linger against mine. "Never be afraid to tell me what you want. You're my wife. My partner. After this movie and the next, every project I do will be a decision we'll make together. Wherever I have to go, you're always welcome."

A small tear forms in the corner of my eye and he wipes it away. "You're so beautiful, Joey. I tried to deny my feelings. I tried to fight every single one of them, but every touch, every kiss, and every time you would look at me it would chip away at my resolve. I thought I could kiss you and enjoy the days we were spending together, but every single one sealed our fate. There was no way I was leaving that house without you next to me."

21

"But you did," I stupidly remind him, ruining the moment.

"It's a mistake I'll never make again."

While we dress for dinner, Josh gives me the rundown on what to expect. He says most of the paparazzi will be gone, having moved on to the next celebrity, but some will linger around, waiting for us to make another appearance.

He asked me from the get-go if I wanted to order room service or venture out and I chose the latter. Not because I don't want to be holed up with my husband, but because I felt like if we didn't leave we'd never eat any food, and we're both famished. We need food in our systems, good food at that, and room service isn't always reliable when it comes to quality.

I put on a simple blue dress with matching heels. It was hanging in the closet and Josh said the manager likely sent it up as a gift. It would be rude not to wear it. Josh dresses in relaxed jeans and a button down, rolling up his sleeves and showing off his arm-porn. He catches me licking my lips as he flexes absentmindedly.

"We can stay in," he reminds me, causing me to avert my eyes.

"No, we need to eat and you know as well as I do if we stay here we'll end up rolling around in our food and not eating it."

Josh comes to stand behind me, nipping at my neck. "And what's wrong with rolling around in a little chocolate pudding?"

"You're insatiable."

"I am, and it's all your fault. I can't get enough of you and I don't want to share you with anyone else." He grinds into my backside, showing me just how much my words ring true.

"Maybe we should go downstairs to the hotel restaurant. That way the manager will see that I'm wearing his gift. The last thing I want to do is upset him."

"I like that idea. Being in good graces with hotel managers is beneficial to us, especially when we want to escape. Plus, that means if we stay in, there will be no paparazzi trying to take our picture. I really like that idea, Mrs. Wilson."

My knees go weak when he refers to me as Mrs. Wilson. I lean my head back onto his shoulder, giving him ample space to continue his beautiful assault on my neck.

"If we're living in L.A., would we really escape to a hotel?" I've read the tabloid reports before—celebrities coming in and out of hotels and calling it a getaway—but if you live there, why would you need to?

"Depending on what's going on in your life, the media could be hounding you and sometimes you just want a break. Hotels offer security, seclusion, and other amenities you might not get at home. Most have state-of-the art gyms, spas, and other services."

"I guess that makes sense."

Josh stands behind me and we regard our reflections in the mirror. Aside from the obvious physical changes—like both our hair being longer and Josh sporting a nice scruff— we're the same people that we were inside the house.

"I think I could look at you all day and never tire of it."

"I think that would be creepy, but I'd still like it. That means our roles would be reversed. I will have gone from the stalker to the stalked," I tell him, taking a jab at my own infatuation with him.

"President of *my* fan club, remember?" He winks, reminding me of the job title that he bestowed upon me in the house.

"Is this a paid position?" I ask, turning in his arms. I let my fingers drift along his cheekbones, tickling the pads of my fingers with his whiskers.

"You don't have to work, Joey. I'll take care of you. I already told you earlier that I want you to travel with me. I don't want to be one of those couples that are separated by distance and plagued by rumors. If we're together, we're stronger than being apart."

I hadn't thought about not working, or needing to find a job in Los Angeles. His words give me a sense of relief all while making me feel happy. I want to be with him, and if that means living out of a hotel for however long it takes, so be it. As long as we're together, I'll be happy.

CHAPTER
four

Josh

As we touch down at the Jack-Edwards Airport, I figure now is the best time to let her know that *Sweet Home Alabama* wasn't exactly filmed here. That has to be one of the hardest parts as an actor when it comes to locations. You read a script and the writers' notes tell you where the film is based, you get excited and look up what the town is like and try to picture yourself as your character walking down the street, only to find out you're not actually filming there, but one or two states away because it's cheaper and the tax credits are higher. In Hollywood it's all about the most bang for your buck.

The same can be said about book adaptations. They're never the same. People are either going to love the book and hate the movie or vice versa. Personally, I love both, especially when they're different.

Walking through the airport without a security detail is risky, but I figured no one here would really care. I was wrong. Maybe it's the drawback of first class. Sure, we get on first and get free cocktails, but getting off the plane first in this situation is backfiring. It didn't take long, maybe a minute or less, for someone to recognize ... *Joey*. Not me, but my wife. And while I filled with pride and my ego swelled because Joey is fucking gorgeous, I feared the onslaught that was about to ensue.

Within seconds we were swarmed, stranded out in the middle of the concourse, surrounded by restaurants without a desk agent in sight. Even as I held her tight and tried to push my way through the crowd we weren't getting anywhere.

That's when we were saved by the airport transit who all but ran people over in order to get to us. Once we hopped on, the fans groaned in unison, making it sound like they were growling. Growling! Who the hell growls at people in the airport?

"Thank you," I say to the driver.

"No worries, man," he replies in a thick Jamaican accent. Hearing him speak gives me another idea for a vacation with Joey. We need a real honeymoon at some tropical island where no one can bother us. I want the seclusion of a private beach without prying eyes and a damn camera.

"Is it always like that?" Joey asks as she nestles into my side. I can feel her heart beating rapidly and mentally kick my own ass for not thinking things through.

"No and that's my fault. I forgot about the show being recently aired and didn't think we'd need any security. It won't happen again." I pull her closer, angling my body toward her, and kiss her on her forehead. Even now that we're on the transport, people are taking videos and pointing at us.

Once we get to baggage claim, airport security is there to meet us, as well as our driver. Of course, the sign welcoming me to Alabama isn't helping matters. Maybe it's time I develop an alias and start traveling under that. If I do, I want something cool that makes people do a double take.

We're taken right out to the car, with our bags already

secured by security, and finally closed in once the door slams shut. The quiet is somewhat comforting, but the agitated state my wife is in isn't.

"I'm sorry. I wasn't thinking."

"It's fine, Josh." Placing her hand on my cheek, she pulls me into a kiss. "I wasn't mentally prepared and I should've been. I've seen the crazy pictures coming from LAX. I guess I didn't think it'd happen at all the airports."

"Can I point out that it was *you* that got us noticed? Not me!" I jab myself in my chest to send the point home, but all she does is laugh.

"Does that make you jealous?"

"Hell no. I only worry about how you're going to react."

"I got this," she says, gracing me with a beautiful smile. "I knew what to expect, and now that I've seen it firsthand I'll be more prepared."

The driver pulls us into the car rental location and helps us with our bags. At the counter, we hand over our driver's licenses and wait.

"We need to change yours," I tell Joey.

Joey looks at me with the most serious expression I have ever seen. "What if I don't want to change my name? The producers never even asked if I wanted to take my 'husband's' last name. I mean can you imagine if you had the last name Hoey and now I'd be Joey Hoey?"

"Are you saying you don't want to be Joey Wilson?" As much as I try to hide the hurt in my voice, I can't and it's stupid. I never wanted to be married in the first place, but now that I am, now that I've had her in my life for the past four, almost five months I want her to be a Wilson. I want the world to know that she's mine.

Her face morphs into a huge smile causing my heart to beat faster. "I'm just giving you a hard time. I think once I have a permanent address I can get my license changed."

Draping my arm around her shoulder, I shake my

head. "I have a feeling you're going to keep me on my toes." Maybe that's the key to a happy marriage: the jokes, pranks, and reminding ourselves that we can't take everything so seriously.

When we're finally on the road and heading toward Daphne, I drop the bomb. "So you know how you love *Sweet Home Alabama?*"

Her eyes light up, instantly making me feel like a dick. "Yes, such a sweet second chance love story and Josh Lucas …" She sighs, making me feel about ten inches tall.

"Do you have something for actors named Josh?"

"Yes, but just one mostly. Wilson's his last name. Have you heard of him?" She winks and I can't fight the shit-eating grin that spreads across my face. I've never felt this way before when receiving a compliment from a beautiful woman. Maybe it's because I always thought there were ulterior motives and they were only saying these things to get something from me. It's not like that with Joey. Every time she compliments me, it feels genuine.

"You're a smooth talker, Mrs. Wilson. Anyway, your favorite movie wasn't exactly filmed here. There are a few scenes, but most of it was filmed in Georgia." I try to watch for her reaction and notice that her mouth drops open and shuts quickly.

"Hollywood is such a lie."

I laugh because it's true. "I know. I'm sorry that I'm killing all the magic for you."

"Eh, it's okay. So you're filming in Daphne, which is where *my* movie was 'filmed', but where is yours based out of?"

"Some coastal town in Texas," I tell her, trying to recall from my script.

"Unbelievable," she says, laughing.

The drive is only about an hour from the airport to the hotel, but it ends up taking us almost three. We decided to drive along the coastal line as much we could, stopping in as many towns as possible so we can sightsee, capture memories on our phones, and make out under the Spanish moss covered oak trees like the newlyweds we are.

When we finally pull into our hotel, we're both tired from traveling. I shouldn't be staying in Daphne, but I want to be close to Joey and the thought of having to drive or be driven an hour or so away to some ritzy ass hotel doesn't appeal to me. It's my hope that our location can remain on the down-low so we can enjoy our time together.

"Don't feed the alligators?" Joey slams the car door and points to the sign, her eyes wide with a mix of terror and 'what the fuck'.

"You're in the south. Stay out of the water unless it's a pool and you can see the water clearly."

"But alligators, Josh? Come on? What if one comes ashore and tries to eat me?"

I laugh. "The likelihood is rare. Alligators only attack if provoked. If you stay out of their habitat, they'll leave you alone."

Joey checks us in while I hang back in the shadows. We're hoping that because the room has been booked under her maiden name, no one will recognize her. Once she has our keys, we take the short elevator right to the third floor where we have booked one of their larger suites. If we're going to live here for a few months, we need some comfort. Sadly for me, my idea of comfort doesn't seem to match that of the hotel.

"Well this isn't fancy," I mutter, dropping our bags on the floor.

"It's perfect." Joey walks past me and goes right to the window. "We have a view of the alligators. It'll be a joy watching them," she says sarcastically.

When I come and stand behind her, I immediately spot one in the water. I don't know if she sees it or not, and I'm not planning on pointing it out to her. "You know," I begin as I kiss her neck, "I won't be working every day and my hours will shift, so we can do a lot together. You won't always be by yourself. And as long as you're not pretending to be Captain Hook, you'll be fine."

"If I'm Captain Hook, are you my Peter Pan?" she asks, turning in my arms.

"I'd rather you be my Tinkerbell," I tell her as I capture her lips.

Whenever I'm on vacation, or even when I've just finished a film, I like to sleep in. It's a luxury that I often don't have. When I'm not working, I'm still up early and hitting the gym to stay in shape.

But as the sun rises and Joey sleeps in my arms, I'm staring into the morning sun. In our haste last night, we forgot to close the blinds and now I'm paying for it dearly. Tilting my head, I see the red digital number displaying a six and that's enough to tell me it's too early to even function. Next week my first call time is at the crack of dawn to film a scene on the beach. The thought of having to change my sleeping habits is enough to make me groan internally.

When Joey stirs I roll us over so I'm lying on top of her. Her arms envelope me, making me feel secure. I can't believe I almost lost her and all because of Jules, although she can't be blamed entirely. I've always had a hard time saying no to Jules. That was until I met Joey and realized my future was a reality television show and the person I was partnered with lit up my life with a smile.

"I want cake," I whisper against her skin. She laughs a groggy, sleep-filled laugh.

"You'll have to wait until we get home." Her fingers push through my hair, each pass almost lulling me back to sleep.

"Home," I say, and that's when a light bulb goes off. I sit up as much as I can without leaving her arms. "We should buy a house." My sleeping wife one-eyes me before trying to tug me back down to her chest. "I'm serious, Joey. I live in a small, two-bedroom apartment and you live with your parents. We need our own place without roommates, parents, and all the other riff-raff that comes with my baggage. We need something that is our own where we buy a hodgepodge of furniture and make love in every room."

This time she's fully awake and looking at me. "Isn't there some law that we have to have nice furniture for when *People* magazine comes to interview you?"

"I didn't say it wasn't going to be nice. I just said we could be different. I don't want a theme. I want people to come into our home and feel welcomed, like they can sit and not worry about ruining something. I want a home, Joey. Not a structure with walls and uneasy feelings."

She smiles brightly. "Okay, we'll buy a house when we get back to Los Angeles."

"It doesn't even have to be there," I tell her, nestling back into her arms.

"It needs to be where you are, Josh. I don't want to be far from you," she says quietly as sleep begins to find her again.

"I feel the same way, Joey. I feel the same way." I close my eyes and try to find a little more shut-eye before we start our first day as tourists. It's my plan to see as much of the area as I can, or find a nice secluded place where I can make love to her all day before I start work and my days are filled with film crews, memorized lines, and acting like I'm in love with someone I'm not.

CHAPTER
five

Joey

After stopping in all the small towns on the way to Daphne from the airport, I suggested Josh take the highway to Orange Beach. I didn't want to be tempted to stop again and really wanted to sink my toes into the sand and relax in his arms under our private cabana.

The reservations were made under my name, as we've decided to use it as long as possible until people realize we're here and start hounding him. Josh reminds me that I'll be the subject of a lot of scrutiny once the media gets wind that I'm with him. I can handle it; at least I think I can. I suppose nothing prepares you for people following you around taking your picture, or stopping you on the street and asking for a selfie. One thing Josh has promised me is that when we're eating dinner, he won't engage fans, but asked that I understand that when shopping or walking down the street with him it's a different story. I get it. He doesn't want to ruin the fan base, and if I saw him trotting along I'd be asking for a picture too. It's in our nature, I think as a fan. As much as I love being with him, I know there are going to be times when I hate his career. Even as a fan I fantasized about being with him. Being there with the glitz and glamour, standing proud next to him as our photos are being taken. And now that I know him and have had a taste with the spotlight, I can't see how the spouses don't crack under pressure.

Love conquers all, though, and that's the motto I'm going to live by.

Absentmindedly, my hand slips into his as I stare out the window at the passing cars. Young women, with the tops to their cute little cars down, are oblivious of the fact that I'm holding hands with Joshua Wilson. I have no doubt in my mind that if they could see through the tinted windows their phones would be out and all sense of responsibility would be lost as they try and snap a picture of him.

"What are you thinking about?" he asks as he exits the highway. Right before my eyes is the most pristine waters I have ever seen. I know they're not best, but seeing the white sands and the crystal blue waters is enough to make me catch my breath. I've always loved the ocean, but now it's going to have a different meaning, being here with Josh on our honeymoon.

"Nothing in particular."

"Must've been something because I saw you frown."

Did he? Was he paying that close attention to me while I was daydreaming?

Glancing over at him, I smile. "I was remembering a time when I fantasized about being with you, like this." I hold up our conjoined hands. "And now I'm wondering if it's just a dream."

He picks up our joined hands and kisses mine, then places them back on his lap and continues to navigate to the parking lot. "We spent ninety-days locked in a house together. I hope by now you've come to terms that this is real and I want to be with you."

"But you hate marriage," I blurt out without thinking. His aversion to marriage has never left my mind. In fact, thoughts of him deciding this isn't for him plague me. Will I wake up one day and find his bags packed by the door with a somber expression on his face, telling me he's leaving? Or better yet, will he cheat because that is the example his parents set for him? My parents have a happy marriage, but it's not without trials and tribulations. I remember them fighting a lot when I was younger, but they never seemed to stay angry at each other for long and I always went to bed with the image of my mom wrapped in my dad's arms.

After turning off the car, Josh angles his body as much as he can to look at me. His fingers caress my cheek and a shy smile plays along my lips as he does. I can't help but lean into his touch and wonder if this feeling will ever go away.

"I did, and I probably still do, but you make everything seem effortless. Maybe it's the newness of being in love or the fact that you and I connected on a different level. I don't know, but I don't want this feeling to go away. When I try to look at the future, you're standing by my side. There were many nights that I laid awake with you sleeping on my chest, and wondered what it was going to be like outside the house with you not next to me. Each time, my heart ached, Joey. And that was something I didn't like feeling."

He leans toward me and I meet him halfway. When our lips touch, it feels like it's the first time again. Everything I felt on stage comes rushing back and I find myself holding him to my lips longer, afraid of letting the memory go. The rush of excitement, the lights and the audience are on instant replay as his lips move softly along mine.

When we break for air, he whispers, "Wow." And I know he felt it, too.

He kisses me again, quickly, before exiting the car and running in front of it and to my door. It's funny, I never expected him to be a gentleman, especially considering he has people that do these things for him, but he is and I like it a lot. When I was with my ex, he didn't hold the door or rush ahead to open it. He lagged back and waited for me to open it. I was annoyed at first, but grew accustomed to just doing it myself. I suppose that should've been my first sign that we were doomed.

With his hand held out to me, he helps me out of the car. Josh plants a kiss right on my lips, out in the open for everyone to see.

"I'm going to go check us in," I tell him breathlessly. Maybe we should've stayed in the hotel for another day before venturing outside. I like the idea of being wrapped in his arms, but I also like the thought of being outside and frolicking in the water with him.

Once we are checked in, the cabana boy—*no, that's not his official title*—takes us to where we're going to be staying. It's private in the sense that no one can see into our cabana unless they're walking by, but definitely wide open in the aspect that the beach is public. Josh thanks him and gives him a tip.

"Do you think he recognized you?" I ask as I set out our beach towels on the chaise lounges.

"If he did, he won't say anything. Most places like to keep their reputation of being a place celebrities can visit. It'd suck if I posted something negative."

"Would you do that?" I inquire. I'm curious to know if it's something he'd do if our location were outted.

"Depends. Here, probably not. We're out in public and it's to be expected, although not from an employee. If we were somewhere private, yes, I'd expect complete anonymity."

"Should I expect the same?"

"Absolutely," he says, pulling me into his arms. "If you decide to go to the spa, I would expect them to treat you better than they treat me."

My fingers play with the ends of his hair. It's surreal to

think that his name gives me any sort of power in the circle of Hollywood. I don't even know how I'd go about using it for something like that.

"You're my wife and everyone knows it. When you call to make a hair appointment, or schedule a manicure, these places aren't going to tell anyone. They're used to keeping their client lists to themselves."

"It's so strange."

"You'll get used to it, but what you won't get used to is this." Josh suddenly scoops me in his arms and an errant squeal escapes through my parted lips. I expect him to toss me onto the chaise, but instead he takes off running toward the ocean.

"Josh, put me down," I demand as my grip on his shoulders becomes deadly. I close my eyes, fearing what is about to come. As soon as I hear the splashing, I brace myself by holding my breath.

If I'm expecting for him to launch into the water, I'm surely mistaken. Instead, he submerges both of us, never letting me go. The water envelops me and while it's cold, being in his arms is all the warmth I need.

"You surprise me every day, Joshua."

"Good, I don't want to be predictable."

We stay in each other's arms, or within arms' reach, splashing each other until other beachgoers arrive. It's nice that they're focused on their own tasks instead of looking at us. I know it's only a matter of time before he's recognized, but hopefully when it happens they will leave us alone.

When we finally head back to our cabana, strawberries and champagne have been delivered. The note on the platter reads, "Welcome, Newlyweds."

"They know who you are," I say to Josh as I hand him the note.

"No, they know who *we* are, Joey, and it's time that you accept it. We're a package deal. You spent three months on a television show, people recognize you now. Reality stars are big news. It's not like you had little airtime or were only shown for five minutes of an hour-long show. With or without me, you're recognizable."

"Oh," I say, unable to form a coherent sentence after his rant.

"You're Joey Wilson. It's time to embrace it."

"So does that mean I get your credit card?" I start to laugh immediately after the words tumble out of my mouth. I didn't mean it to sound like I want to spend his money. I don't. I can earn my own and still plan to.

"Yes, but it will have your name on it. I've already ordered it."

"You did? When?"

He motions for me to sit down, but instead of sitting across from him, I sit next to him so we can face each other.

"Before I asked you to marry me again."

"What if I had said no?"

He shrugs and instead of answering right away, he gives me a glass of champagne and brings a strawberry to my lips. I bite, taking my time to push through the sweet fruit. Josh lets out an audible growl, causing me to laugh.

"Even if you had said no, I had no intention of filing the paperwork until we had a chance to spend some time together. I knew how you felt about me ... hell, how you feel about us, and wanted to fight for a chance with you."

I take a drink of the champagne, letting the cool bubbly liquid tickle its way down my throat. "I wouldn't have spent your money."

"I know, but it would've been there for you if you needed it."

The fact that he did this isn't lost on me. I know I'm entitled to his earnings—maybe not what he's done prior to our marriage, but everything coming up—and knowing that makes me ill. I would never take advantage of him like that.

If he were to file for divorce, as he originally planned early on, I would've been fine. Albeit, heartbroken.

"Do you want me to sign a pre-nup?"

Blanching at my question, he shakes his head. Josh downs his glass of champagne and finishes mine for me also. I want to balk, but the seriousness I see on his face tells me I shouldn't say anything.

Josh kisses me; his cold tongue tastes fruity, and it's very inviting. Before I realize what's happening, we're on our sides with my leg between his and our lips moving aggressively against each other's.

"What's mine is yours. Tonight when we get back to the hotel, I'll show you everything. You can see all my earnings, and what I have in the pipeline."

"Josh, I don't need to see all of that."

"You're my partner, Joey, and I'm going to want your opinion on scripts. Plus, you need to know how much to spend when looking for a house for us."

"A house?"

He shrugs. "Or maybe a condo. I'm not too keen on the idea that I'll be on location and you'll be home, waiting for me. Selfishly, I'd rather have you in a hotel waiting for me to come back every night."

"I'll be wherever you want me to be."

He smiles before kissing me into oblivion. I don't want this euphoria to go away, but know deep in my heart it will if we're not careful.

CHAPTER
six

Josh

Being on set right now sucks. It's not that I hate my job because I don't. I love what I do and am blessed to have a talent that pays me well. It's just that I want to be someplace else and making this movie is the last thing I want to be doing right now. The timing is bad, but I had no idea that spending my summer in a house, married to someone that I'd fall in love with, would put a wrench into my plans. I want to whisk Joey away to some island, where her and I can just be us and not worry about anything, but I can't. I'm filming back-to-back movies and it'll be months before we're able to go away and spend quality time with each other.

The worst part about this whole situation was leaving Joey's warm arms at the crack-ass of dawn and walking into a hot and humid trailer. I didn't even bother anyone with a hello when I arrived on set, I just yelled out asking why the air conditioner wasn't on because I was angry that my life isn't going the way I want it to right now. It's not even that hot, but between the thicker air and my frustration of having to end my honeymoon, it's the only thing I could think of to let people know I'm not happy.

Without any more provocation on my part, the AC was flipped on, even though I probably could've done without it at four in the morning. I'm not sure what the director is thinking, starting us off on a sunrise scene, but whatever. They get paid the big bucks for their creative vision, not me.

"Sit here," an overly eager and far too peppy woman with a headset on, who appears out of nowhere, barks orders at me. I'm willing to bet she was the one who flipped the switch on the air conditioner, as she's the only other person in my trailer. She's telling people what to do through her microphone and pointing in every direction even though there isn't another person in sight. To my knowledge I'm the only one in here right now unless I'm sharing. And if that's the case, Matt and I will be having words very shortly.

"Here's your schedule for the day, along with your lines broken out per scene. You need to be in make-up in five." With that she storms out, slamming the door behind her, and continues to yap into her headset. I go over the stack of papers, rereading the lines that I've already committed to memory. Even though I know them, I'll refresh my memory before every scene because I know I'm likely to forget since my head isn't in it right now.

As soon as I step outside, I wish for the cool air in my trailer. People with the same disgruntled look that I'm wearing, filter around mumbling incoherent sentences as they hustle to do their jobs. I've always said that one day I want to do each job on a movie set, but I never get the time and no one ever takes me seriously. Most A-list stars think I'm crazy when I say that, brushing me off as if I'm trying to prove something. I'm not. I'm trying to learn the craft because my good looks will only get me so far until the next young stud comes along. I need a backup plan. Everyone has to start and even finish somewhere, and while some were born into the industry, or happened to hit it big with one movie, I'm paving my way with each movie I'm in.

I realize as I walk into the make-up trailer I have no idea who my co-star is. The correspondence I had with Matt about this movie was that I refused to work with Jules. I never did follow up and see if the female lead was changed. I suppose once I find out who I'm working with, it will determine if I'm even staying on this film or not. For all I know Matt didn't take it seriously and Jules is still starring opposite me.

I grab the first chair I see and sit down, letting the ladies get to work. One does my hair, while the other focuses on my make-up. It's a hazard of the job and one that I loathe. I don't know how women do it every day when the constant feeling that something is on your face drives me crazy. That is one of the things I love most about Joey. She's not afraid to go without make-up.

"Well, you don't need much," the girl says as the brush moves over my face. "You've been tanning, I see."

"The sun does wonders."

"You should use sunblock," she counters.

"You're right and I do, but even that doesn't always help."

"Please take off your shirt." She states it as if this is an every day occurrence for us.

"Excuse me?"

With a huff, she turns her back to me. I can see her reflection in the mirror as she looks down at her palette of make-up.

"Your scene is shirtless. I need to make sure your skin isn't blotchy."

I do as she says, placing my shirt on the counter in front of me.

"What is that?" The make-up artist points to a red spot that sits on my pec. I look down and rub my hand over the spot, remembering very clearly how it got there. Joey and I had just finished parasailing and were back in our cabana having a little fun. One thing led to another and she ended up biting me hard, leaving a mark. I happen to like it.

"An imprint of my wife's teeth."

The soulless eyes of my make-up artist try to burn a hole through my head. The way she looks at me should be enough to send me into a mess of tears while cowering in the corner.

"You have a shirtless shoot and you let some woman dig her teeth into your skin?"

For the first time in my career I'm faced with having to bite my tongue. Or maybe I shouldn't. No one should speak about my wife, in any way, ever. Often I'd hear people talk about Jules and it bothered me, but not enough to say anything. With Joey, it's different. I'm different.

"Let's be very clear on one thing here, *that* woman is my wife and you will respect her whether she's standing in this room or not. If she wants to leave her mark on me, then so be it. It's your damn job to cover it up, and if that isn't something you're capable of doing I have no doubts you can be easily replaced." I'm surprised by my tone. I never raised my voice, but made sure she understood me clearly. The hair stylist behind me never says a thing, even though she paused with her fingers in my hair. It's slightly awkward, but I get it.

"It'll take time."

"Not my issue," I remind her as I sit back in the chair and let them do their thing. If I thought she was going to be gentle, I was sadly mistaken. She took every opportunity to dig into my skin that she could, making sure I was well aware how angry she is that she had to work extra at covering up the blemish. *Next time she should ask me if I care … not that there'll be a next time for her on any film I'll be working on in the future.*

"Hello," I call out as soon as I open the door to our suite. Soft music plays from behind our bedroom door. I follow the sound to the bathroom and peek in. My wife is encased in bubbles with headphones on and her lips are moving to whatever song she's listening to. All I can think about is how my life is playing out in the movies. I'm in Alabama where her favorite movie is based out of and she's playing Julia Roberts in the bathtub like *Pretty Woman*, minus the hooker part. This better have a happy fucking ending because after today I'm going to need one.

I contemplate letting her know I'm here or just start taking my clothes off. My dick is already straining against my pants, begging to be free and buried inside of her. The water splashing catches my attention and when I look, she's eyeing me.

"Hey," I say, stepping into the bathroom.

Joey moves to the edge and pulls off her headphones.

"Hi." Her voice is sweet and soothing, something I missed all day. I thought I'd have time to call her, but I didn't even have time to take a leak or grab food. Work was constant because my new co-star has to report to college for her last semester of classes so the director wants to get all her scenes done as soon as possible.

Bending down on my knees, I capture her lips with mine. I've missed the taste of her mouth and how she makes me feel like everything is right in the world. The attraction I feel for her is surpassing anything I have ever felt before.

Joey grabs at the buttons on my jeans and quickly works her hand inside my pants, pushing them down as much as she can over my hips. My cock jumps with anticipation knowing he's about to get lucky.

Slipping off my shirt and losing the jeans, shoes, and

socks, I step into the garden tub. The water is still hot and slightly burns my skin.

"How long have you been in here?"

"Only a few minutes."

I pull her to me, unable to refrain from having her near me. Joey straddles me, the water sloshing around us. You would think that we'd avoid being in the tub or shower since this is the only place we could be alone while we were in the house, but yet here we are.

Her breasts are covered in soapy suds, making it hard for me to see her taut nipples, and before I can do anything about it, she leans forward and moves her wet body along mine. In an instant I'm hard and wanting to be inside of her.

"I missed you today," I tell her, losing my fucking man card once and for all. All these emotions that she's bringing out of me are hard to cope with, but necessary. With Jules I always felt detached, afraid to show her how I felt, but with Joey I can't help it.

"Show me how much," she all but begs as she continues to slide up and down my body. I don't have to do anything when she centers herself, except guide her hips.

"This … this is what I've needed all day." The words are choppy, but I manage to spit them out. Each thrust brings me deeper inside of her until I can't take it anymore. Screwing in the water isn't always the best.

"Come here," I tell her as I try to maneuver us to sit on the edge. Joey follows quickly, wasting no time to straddle me. She cries out when I enter her, moving slowly until I'm fully sheathed. The lack of lubrication is not our friend right now.

"Does this hurt?"

She shakes her head, biting her lower lip. "It'll be fine in a second."

I brush my thumb against her clit as she moves up and down my shaft. My head rolls back when I feel her starting to get wet and her movements pick up.

"Oh God," she moans as I bite down on her nipple and her nails dig into my back. I shouldn't think about it, but the thought crosses my mind on how the make-up artist is going to feel tomorrow when she sees the scratches on my back. Thing is, I don't give a flying fuck. If Joey wants to bite, pinch, and rip my skin apart, so be it. To me that means I'm doing my damn job and pleasing her.

"Best fucking welcome home I've ever had," I tell her as my hands find her hips and help her thrust.

"I've thought about you all day."

"I can't wait for you to tell me all about it."

I pick her up and place her on the counter, and as soon as I see myself in the mirror I know I want something different. Pulling out and lifting her up, I turn her so she can see, too.

"Watch while I fuck you."

I push in slowly, watching as her eyes roll back in her head. For a moment I stare at my dick as it moves in and out of her, lost in the moment that I can do this every day with her as long as she'll have me.

When I meet her gaze in the mirror I lose all train of thought about seduction and fuck the shit out of her. Her eyes tell me that this is what she wants, and when I see her hand splayed out on the bathroom mirror with her lip between her teeth I know I'm doing my job as her husband.

CHAPTER
seven

Joey

I thought I wouldn't have any issues finding stuff to do while Josh was on set, but that's a giant lie. My life is boring and I often find myself staring out my hotel bedroom window waiting for an alligator to pop out of the water and scare some unsuspecting tourists. Sadly, it never happens, or if it does it's when I'm sitting here wallowing in self-pity.

I'm a supportive wife, I am. I love that he loves his job and I love him for it, but this shit is for the birds. I miss my friends, the comfort of home, and freedom. Not that I've been hounded by anyone, but that hasn't stopped me from looking over my shoulder or making sure I'm wearing a ball cap and sunglasses when I step outside to go shopping. I almost wish someone would take my photo so I would have something to read online. Browsing the web for set photos has become a chore and seeing Josh with another woman sort of hits home. I know it's all part of his job, but that doesn't mean I have to like it.

My phone rings and I fly across the room to answer it, hoping it's Josh. When he's on set, his free time is so limited because of his co-star that he's unable to call. He's complained that this is the fastest he's ever filmed a movie and the director has made some comments about it. Josh knows it's his fault because he refused to work with Jules, which makes me love him even more.

"Hey, Joey."

"Millie! Oh my God, how are you?"

I feel like I've failed her as a friend. I know she's been going through a lot and maybe I should've set some time aside to chat with her more.

"I'm good, but morning sickness is kicking my ass."

"I'm sorry, Millie. The baby is doing good though, right?"

She sighs. "Yeah, the baby is fine."

"And Cole?"

This time there's a long pause and my heart falls. I thought, out of all of us, that Cole and Millie would be the ones to make it. Hell, at this point I'm not even sure Josh and I will last a year. It's shitty to think it, but something tells me that I need to always be on my toes where my marriage is concerned.

"He's—" She doesn't finish before a sob breaks out. I want to go to her, console her, but I don't want to leave Josh.

"I'm sorry, Millie. I don't know what else to say."

"Do you think Josh could talk to him?"

"Yeah … I mean, I can ask him." It's not the answer I want to give, but she's alone and pregnant. "He's going to want to know what's going on, though, and you haven't exactly told me."

She sniffles and I can hear tissues rustling in the background. "His mom … she hates me and I don't know why. I'm a good person, Joey. I am, but she … she's evil and has made my life a living hell. This past month I've done nothing but cry and I finally broke down and told Cole that he needs to decide if he wants to be in my life or if he's going to let his mother dictate everything for him. He chose her. He told me that the show was a mistake and that he wished he never did it. It's like she's brainwashed him against me."

Wow! I know at one point in my life I thought this, too, but never said it out loud to anyone. The day I heard Jules laughing in the room was the day I regretted everything. If it weren't for Bronx, I would've run, but he convinced me to go through the media junket during the weeks after the show and to handle mine and Josh's issues privately. Smartest thing I ever did. Not because it led me back to Josh, but because it didn't tarnish any reputations.

"Millie, I don't know what to say."

"Me neither. I mean, it's a good thing I can afford to have this baby on my own and I can still work, but I'm going to be regulated to a desk job until after I give birth."

"Maybe she's crooked."

"What?"

"His mother. Maybe she's up to no good and that's why she doesn't like you. Think about it, Millie. You're a police officer and most mothers would welcome a career woman into their home. Not only that, but Cole loves you and that alone would at least make her warm up to you. But to flat out dis you, and for Cole to take her side is fishy. I'd run a background check on her and see what you find."

"Have you been watching a lot of television?"

"Yes," I laugh. "I know what you're thinking, but just humor me. I'll still have Josh call Cole, but do this to entertain me. I'd rather think she's an evil mastermind than to shun her unborn grandchild. As for Cole, she must be holding something over his head for him to choose her over you and the baby. I saw him in the house. Hell, we all did. That man was smitten from the word go, so there has to be something in the background."

She sniffles and laughs at the same time. "You're crazy."

"I know. Plus, I'm bored out of my freaking mind here."

"Do you stay in the hotel all day?"

Yes, but I don't tell her that. "Sometimes. We're near the beach and I go there often to read, but when it comes to exploring I wait for Josh. I want to share it with him. He thought he'd be around more, but his co-star has to go back to school or something so they shoot longer hours to accommodate her schedule."

"And screw up your honeymoon?"

"Not necessarily. He's in my arms each night. Exhausted or not, he's at least holding me until he has to get up and go back to work."

"Have you been on set? Is it magical?"

I can't help but laugh and wonder if I should burst her bubble about Hollywood and their fake magic. I decide that under the circumstances she needs to continue to believe it. "Not yet, probably in the next few days."

"I can't wait to hear about it. Okay," she says, sighing, "I'm going to look his mother up and see what she's about. I can't believe I'm going to do this."

I clap my hands with excitement. "I'll be waiting. Call me as soon as you find something! And when I see Josh tonight, I'll ask him to call Cole."

"Love you, Joey."

"Love you, too, Millie. It'll work out. I have a good feeling."

We hang up and I fight the wave of emotions that are trying to sneak up on me. I can't compare their relationship to Josh's and mine. We aren't pregnant, nor do we have parental involvement hanging over our heads. His parents probably don't even know he's married, while mine are eagerly planning a massive reception for when he's done filming. The difference in our parents is night and day.

Only minutes after I hang up with Millie, I hear the door open. I sit up with my heart racing, waiting to see if I'm about to be mugged or if by chance my husband is home early.

"Did you get fired?" I ask, as I run across the room and jump into his arms. He catches me effortlessly, letting the door slam shut behind him.

"No, although sometimes I wish. My scenes are done for the day. Once I did my last cut, I hightailed it out of there so fast I don't think they realize I'm gone."

"And you came right home to me."

"Why wouldn't I?" He looks confused by my statement—as he should be. He sets us down on the couch, but situates us so that I'm sitting on his lap.

"I didn't mean it the way it sounded. Of course you came right home. You know my mind, it gets carried away sometimes and considering I just got off the phone with Millie … well, let's just say I don't want to go through what she is going through right now."

"Their problems aren't ours, Joey." Josh nestles into my neck and pulls me close.

He's right. I shouldn't let their problems become ours, but she's my friend and my heart hurts for her.

"You're right. I'm sorry."

"Nothing to be sorry for," he murmurs, kissing my shoulder. "What do you say we go out to dinner, maybe do a little dancing?"

I lean my head into him and think that a nap would be just as nice, but getting out of here and being with my husband would be a welcome reprieve.

"I'd love that."

He kisses me again and tells me to get dressed. As I stand, he swats me on my rear before he stands and follows me into the bedroom.

"Josh, this place is amazing."

He somehow found this small little beachside restaurant that has the most perfect ambiance. We're sitting at a table for two outside, under white lights with some music playing in the background.

Once our order is placed, he pours us some wine before taking my hand in his. "Have you thought about a date?" he asks me mid-sip.

I swallow quickly and shake my head. "I haven't. I figured it would need to be around your filming schedule."

"I have another movie after this one, then I'm taking a break. We can have a destination wedding. We can go somewhere like Greece, France, or even Australia. You can invite whomever you want. I'll cover all the expenses. I just want to marry you in front of our friends and family."

I lean forward and push his hair back, away from his eyes. "Josh, we're already married. We can have a reception and eat cake."

Smiling, he meets me the rest of the way to give me a kiss. "I like your cake, Joey. But I want to do this the right way. You need your dream wedding. You deserve the chance to be on that show about picking the right wedding dress. I want to see the excitement in your face when you find the perfect flowers and console you when the band you want isn't available to play. I want you to yell at me when I haven't picked my groomsmen and be there when we test wedding cake."

"Really, you want all of this?"

"I do. I never thought I did, but being with you makes me want to experience the things I've shut myself off to for all these years."

"Why the change, Josh?"

Pulling me to standing, he brings me into his arms. We sway to the music and the waves crashing into the shore. "You've changed me and I can't even try to explain it. All day I find myself thinking about you, wondering what you're doing and getting angry that I'm working and you're not with me. I've already sent Matt a list of demands for the next movie, guaranteed breaks and whatnot so I can talk to you during the day because I miss you. And all of this should scare me because I imagine my parents were like this at one time in their lives, but it all changed. We have to promise each other that when we start sensing that change, we stop what we're doing and make it out first priority to fix it."

"Okay."

"Okay, what?" he asks.

"Okay for everything. We'll set a date. We'll pick a color scheme and location. We'll ask our best friends to be in our wedding, but I draw the line at another television show."

Laughing, Josh pulls me closer. "You know, Barry has been hounding me about doing a show with us. He wants to follow us around."

"I'm boring. I spend most of my days in the hotel room."

"He's a producer, he'd incite drama into our lives and have us fighting over the thread count on our sheets."

"That's stupid."

"It's TV and people at home eat that shit up because it makes us look normal."

"We are normal," I remind him as we continue to sway to the music.

"He'd pay us."

"It's intrusive. We have nothing to show them. Besides, you're working and if I'm not allowed on set, they wouldn't be either so it would be me on the camera all the time. I already did that once in my life."

Josh spins me around, causing me to laugh. "I told him we'd think about it after we got back to Los Angeles."

I look at him questioningly. "What's the difference?"

"We'll have a house. Our lives will be more normal than they are now. And that gives you time to think about it."

Before I can answer, our dinner arrives and we head back to our table. Even as I take the first bite, my stomach rolls. I don't want to do another show, but Josh seems eager to do it and that scares me. The last thing I want is for a crew to follow me around while I'm trying to plan a wedding and find my footing in the Hollywood crowd. I'd rather fail when no one is watching.

CHAPTER
eight

Josh

Leaving Joey every morning is getting harder and harder. I don't know if it's because I'm not into this movie and the fast filming process, if it's because I'm not entirely fond of my demanding co-star, or simply because I'd rather be with Joey. I'm sure it's mostly the latter considering the way she makes me feel. I've never been so comfortable with someone before. I've never not cared that people were taking our photos at dinner because they're capturing moments that we haven't been able to capture outside of our own memories.

Either way, this movie can't be done soon enough. I'm ready to move on, get back to Los Angeles, find a house, and start living a life with her. I know she hates living in the hotel, but it's something she's going to have to get used to. I want her to travel with me, be near me while filming. Being away from her for long periods of time isn't going to work for me. It's selfish of me to say, I know, but it's how I feel. I suppose she can always travel and come visit, but it won't be the same.

Falling asleep and waking up in her arms is the only thing getting me through these shoots.

Finally, my scenes are becoming fewer and I'm allotted more breaks. Each break is spent talking to Joey, and even when it's mindless chatter, hearing her voice helps get me through the rest of my day. I've finally convinced her that she *needs* to leave the hotel, daily. It doesn't matter what she's doing, as long as she's out and about. She's scared to spend my money for fear she'd look like a gold-digger. I get that, but she's my wife and she has to realize sooner or later that what's mine is hers. Joey doesn't have to work if she doesn't want to—in fact, I prefer that she not.

When she tried to talk to me about Cole and Millie, I had to shut her down. I've seen too many couples fight because of what their friends are going through. We both care about our friends, but there has to be a fine line of when to get involved. Since our last appearance, Cole and I haven't spoken. I didn't really expect us to maintain a solid friendship, but knew Millie and Joey would. I get that Joey wants to help them, but it's none of our business. Joey and I are going to have enough of our own issues to deal with once we're back home. The media will be relentless in picking our relationship apart and I'd rather focus all of my energy on making sure Joey knows that I'm in love with her and not some random coffee girl that happens to post a selfie with the wrong caption.

As soon as I finish my current scene I hightail it to my trailer. My phone is sitting there, waiting for me, and in my hand by the time I'm spread out on my sofa.

"Done already?"

There's no sultry hello when she answers and deep down that bothers me. I know I shouldn't look for the worst in everything and give her the benefit of the doubt. Maybe I caught her doing something and she wasn't prepared to answer my video call?

"Hello, wife," I say instead of answering her question. Her

face lights up, quelling any thoughts I had that something may be off.

"Hello, husband," she replies. "I miss you," she adds, instantly putting the cheesiest smile on my face.

"I miss you, too, Joey. I'll be done early. Do you want to grab dinner out?"

"Yes, but dessert back here. I made a cake today."

My stomach rolls angrily, mocking me for being here and not at home with Joey, eating her cake. It's not that she does anything special, it's that she made it. The memory of her smashing still warm cake in my face during the show is as crisp as the day it happened. I thought I was being smooth by bringing up the fact that we hadn't shared our celebratory cake that most newlyweds do at the reception and she took the bait. Only she bested me and I'll never forget it.

"We could always have cake for dinner," I suggest. She laughs, making me wonder how many times in her life she has done that. Growing up, it didn't matter what I ate, as long as I put food in my stomach. Dinners stopped being a thing in my house early on. My mother was too busy with her boy-toys to make dinner and my father was never home on time. I ate whatever I could find: chips, cookies, ice cream, frozen dinners. My lifestyle as a pre-teen was anything less than stellar in the food department.

"We could. How long is your break for?"

"About an hour. Once we hang up, I'm going to take a nap. I did a fight scene today and even the motions of trying to hit someone takes a toll."

"Maybe you need to work out."

"Haha, you're funny," I tell her. I've complained repeatedly that the filming schedule has messed up my exercise routine. In the house, I could lift weights and do cardio every day. I felt great, and I was probably in the best shape of my life. Being on set has ruined that. "Are you saying I'm weak?"

Joey laughs. "Not at all. You can easily carry me around

the suite."

"That's because you're usually attached to my dick and I don't want to pull out."

"Josh …" she warns. We tried the video sex thing the other day and I got caught jacking off by the production assistant. Apparently people don't knock on set here and she caught me with my pants around my ankles, my hand moving fast up and down my shaft and my wife encouraging me via video chat. As if things couldn't get any worse, the assistant didn't even bother to leave the room, instead standing there in shock at what she was witnessing. Joey heard me yelling and she started yelling. It wasn't good.

"I can always go into the bathroom," I tell her, hoping she agrees. "Or you can get yourself off and I'll watch."

"You'll just watch?"

I nod and she rolls her eyes.

"I don't believe you."

"You're probably right. I can't control myself when I'm with you."

"Same here," she says, taking a bite of whatever she's eating. It stupidly makes me long to be that object. Shit, I think I need help. I've never been this attached to someone before. It can't be healthy. I'd ask a friend or two, but most of mine are single, or getting divorced. I don't want to know that these feelings I'm having will wear off, so maybe living in my magic bubble of bliss is what's best for me.

I yawn and rub my hand down my face. The last thing I want to do is hang up with her, but sleep is a hot commodity when filming. The fresher I look, the better it is for me.

"Take a nap, Josh. I'll be here when you get home."

The word home hits hard. The fact that she's calling our suite our home sends a jolt right to my heart. Maybe I've been worrying about nothing.

"I love you," I tell her.

"I love you, too. Kick ass today." She blows me a kiss that

I return and we both hang up. As soon as I roll over and close my eyes the pounding on my door starts. I think about ignoring it, but the knocking becomes incessant.

"What?" I yell out, hoping that whoever is on the other side of the door will ask their question and go away. When they don't say anything I close my eyes again, only for the knocking to start back up.

"You're seriously pissing me off," I yell as I get up. My trailer is small, taking only a few steps until I'm at the door. "*What?*" I shout as I fling it open, immediately regretting answering when I see who's on the other side.

Jules stands there, shocked by my attitude. I don't regret yelling at her because she shouldn't even be here. Her hair is pulled up in a ponytail, something I've never seen her do before, and it makes me wonder if she's trying to emulate Joey's look. She's also lacking a lot of the make-up she usually wears. Aside from the hair and make-up, everything else is still Jules with ridiculous high heels and a trench coat. Red flags go off that whatever she's wearing, or not wearing, under that coat needs to stay there.

"What do you want, Jules? I'm busy." I stand in the doorway, blocking her view from seeing in the trailer. I want her to assume Joey is inside.

"Can I come in?"

I shake my head. "No."

"We need to talk."

"No we don't. I've already told you, we're done and I've moved on." I'd flash her my wedding band, but I've taken it off for filming.

"I get that, Joshie, but we need to talk." That's when she opens her coat and everything around me stands still. Even being fully dressed there are things I can't unsee and this is one of them. The Jules I'm used to is not standing in front of me. This new one is standing here with her normal skintight clothes on, but with the added feature of a protruding belly.

"Now can I come in?" she asks again, this time her voice is soft and pleading. I nod in shock and step aside, letting her walk into my rickety trailer. "I love what you've done to the place," she says, laughing, as she walks around the square box. The trailer isn't much, but while on set it's mine. It serves as my sanctuary, a place where I can get away from it all.

Except now I want to run from it.

"Jules." I try to get her attention, but her back is facing me. I've played this game with her before. She wants me to touch her, pull her to me, and beg her to tell me what's bothering her. I won't this time. I won't do it.

After a minute, she gives up and turns to face me. I remain in my spot, near the door. If I need a quick escape this is my only option.

"Like I said, we need to talk." Smiling, she rubs her hand over her belly. Everything from my throat to my stomach bounces, swells, and tries to rip through my body.

"I don't see how that is any of my concern." I nod toward her stomach.

"Oh, Josh, I think you know why I'm here."

Nope. That is what I tell myself. *I don't and I refuse to believe this has anything to do with me.*

Jules sits down and makes herself comfortable, although I suppose if she actually wore sensible shoes while carrying extra weight around she might fare better. She continues to run her hand over her belly as if it's somehow soothing.

"What do you want, Jules?" I ask for the third time. This time she sets her steely gaze upon me, and smiles one of the most sinister grins I have ever seen in my life.

"You."

"I'm married."

"Doesn't matter. Divorces are easy. Besides, we're going to start a family. Surely your new wife will have an issue with you being tied to another woman for the rest of your life."

"It's not mine, Jules. We haven't been together for

months."

She laughs as if she's mocking me. "I'm almost six months along, you can do the math. I know you're smart enough to figure it all out."

I shake my head, unwilling to acknowledge that this is my fate. I don't want children, even Joey knows this and has accepted it. Hell, being married is a stretch for me, but with Joey it's been worth changing my beliefs.

"How come I'm just hearing about this now? Surely the tabloids would've picked up on what you're trying to hide."

"I've been staying at home, waiting for you to come back to me. I tried telling you after I found out, but you must've blocked my number. I get it, Joshie, I do. She's new, exciting, and probably caters to you. But let's be realistic here, it's always been Josh and Jules, and now that we're having a baby we can go back to the way things used to be."

"That's where you're wrong, Jules," I say, shaking my head. "I'm in love with Joey and there's no room for you in our lives."

She brushes off my statement as if my words don't mean anything. "I'm pregnant and you're the father. I'm fairly certain that cements me in your life whether you and your precious reality TV wife want me there or not."

Jules stands and walks over to me. My heart races with anticipation of what she might try. For years she's been my weakness, my go-to when shit was hard and by my side when things were good. If I hadn't met Joey, I'd probably be back to my on again off again bullshit with Jules.

"You don't want to be like your father, do you, Josh? The absent dad who never paid attention to his son, until his son made a name for himself? You don't want to be a father who never sees their child because your current wife doesn't allow it? How much did you suffer as a child? Are you telling me that you'd do this to your own flesh and blood?"

She has me by the balls, in a tight vise grip. Jules knows

everything about my family and how much I hated growing up with absent parents, which is the main reason I don't want children. Movie sets aren't a place to raise a family and knowing my wife and child are home without me for months on end would kill me. The fact of the matter is, I'd have to be an absent father or quit my job and the latter isn't going to happen. That's one of the reasons why I think it's best for me to never have children.

I swallow hard and refuse to look at Jules. All I can see is Joey, sitting on the couch while I deliver the news to her. I've told her that Jules won't be a problem in our lives and I meant it. Seems to me that I'm a proven liar. Joey can't hold this against me, though, because it happened before I met her.

"Here's the address where I'm staying. You have my number. I don't want things to get ugly, but the media is about to find out that we're expecting."

With that she pushes me out of the way and exits my trailer. Even though she doesn't slam the door, I still jump when I hear it latch and rush to my small bathroom to expel the contents of my stomach. Everything I've worked for, everything that I've achieved with Joey is gone. I don't care how forgiving or accepting she is, Jules has already ruined enough for Joey and this will be the defining moment.

CHAPTER
nine

Joey

After hanging up with Josh I finally decide to heed his words about getting out of the hotel and enjoying myself. It's truly easier said than done, but I'm making an effort, even if the alligator pond freaks me the hell out.

Luckily Josh is picked up every day and taken to set so our rental car is free for me to use, otherwise I'd be hoofing it. Walking does sound better because it affords me the opportunity to stop and smell the roses, but it's unsafe and the last thing I want to do is put myself in danger or upset Josh.

Parking along Main Street, I check out the cute little shops along the road. One is a bridal store that I linger outside the big glass window contemplating whether or not I should go in. I don't know what I'm afraid of with having a real wedding with Josh. We're already married and having a ceremony with our friends and family wouldn't be that big of a deal, except I can't wrap my head around it. Josh doesn't have much in the means of family so why is it so important to have a big wedding? Surely a party would be enough. Maybe he doesn't remember that I planned a wedding before. I was weeks away from getting married, only to have my heart ripped out of my chest. I had the perfect dress, flowers, and location. My honeymoon was planned and apartment ready to move into. Some wounds are hard to get over, but I get where he's coming from. He wasn't a part of that. He's not the one who hurt me.

The door to the store opens and a young woman with her mother come out. In the young woman's arm is a dress bag, but it's her expression that catches me off guard. She's beaming and it's not an ordinary smile. By looking at her, you can tell she's happy—that whatever she's holding in her arms is part of her dream and her mother … well, her smile matches that of her daughters.

Maybe this is what Josh was talking about, the elation that comes with having a wedding. It's something neither of experienced and something I've always dreamt of. I decide to go in and welcome the cool air inside the store. Actually, it's a reprieve to be in air conditioning.

"Hello, how can I help you?"

"Hi," I say, shrugging my shoulders. "I was walking by and saw the store and thought I'd come in and look."

"When's your wedding?"

"We haven't set a date yet." I try to play it off as nonchalantly as possible.

"You're about a six?"

"Sometimes a four." I don't tell her that when it's my time of the month I can push an eight. Thankfully we're not there yet.

"Have a look and let me know what you want to try on. Is it just you?"

I look around, wondering if people followed me in. I nod. "Like I said, this is a spur of the moment browsing session."

The clerk seems to buy my excuse and lets me look

through the gowns without being bothered. The first set that I come to are so intricate and heavy I can't imagine that they're at all comfortable. I think that's what I'd want; something that's comfortable yet drastically different from what I had before.

"Cinderella," I mutter to myself.

"Oh, her dress is over here," the sales clerk speaks up, causing me to jump. She takes my hand, as if we're suddenly best friends, and pulls me toward the back of the store. Before my eyes a dress is pulled from the rack and set out before me.

"This is an off white version which I find a bit classier."

I run my fingers over the beadwork and my hand down over the layers and layers of tulle. I can picture myself being spun around on the dance floor in this dress.

"May I try it on?"

"Of course." She leads me to the dressing room, which is larger than most, and gives me privacy. Once I've stepped into the dress it's like my world has shifted on its axis. "Let me fix the back for you." She appears again, out of thin air, to clamp me into the dress before guiding me out to the pedestal so I can see myself in the wall of mirrors.

I gasp at the vision in front of me. My hair is already up with a few tendrils hanging down, framing my face. The make-up I'm wearing is natural and in soft hues, and my already tanned skin is the perfect tone to make the dress stand out.

"Your fiancé won't be able to take his eyes off of you all night long."

"He's my husband, actually. We sort of eloped and now we're planning a wedding."

The clerk stands behind me, tugging the dress in places, making sure everything is lined up. "Wait, I know you."

As my heart speeds up, I do the only thing I can think and continue to focus on the dress instead of meeting her gaze through the mirror. If I act like it's no big deal, maybe she won't make it one.

"You guys haven't been in the news since you said yes during the *Helen* show. My friends and I thought maybe you changed your mind backstage."

I shake my head and tell her that's not the case.

"What brings you to Daphne?"

"We like the laid back life," I tell her. I imagine people know that movies are filmed here, but maybe not. Either way, I'm not telling her that Josh is here working. The last thing I want is for him to be stalked.

"So you guys are getting married?"

"Again," I tell her, afraid I've already said too much. I can't take it back now, though. If she had recognized me earlier, maybe I'd have been a bit tighter lipped.

"Well I'm happy for you. I watched the show and was rooting for you guys the whole time. Between you and me, I'm so happy he dumped that harlot, Jules Maxwell. She's never been anything but trouble for him."

You and me both, I think, but I can't say it. Even I know when it's best not to comment on Jules. What I say about her in my suite is another story. So I smile softly and pretend to examine the dress a bit more by turning to see the side views.

"You're very beautiful."

"Thanks. I'll take the dress."

"You'll be stunning. Let me get your measurements and we'll have it back to you in six weeks."

"Actually," I say, grabbing her arm before she leaves, "can I just buy it today, as is? I don't know when I'll need it or where I'll be."

Her face falls. I'm sure she was thinking that her store would get some media attention. For all I know she would've had the media here when I came back to pick it up.

"Yes, of course. Go ahead and change and I'll have it packaged up for you."

Once she helps me out of the dress, I give it back to her.

Her earlier cheeriness is gone, making me wonder if I'm right about her wanting some attention or whether it's just my paranoia. After I'm out of the dressing room I head to the counter, lingering around because she's with another client.

"I can ring you up." Another clerk appears and starts typing in the computer. I give her all my information, using the address that Josh gave me. It belongs to his agent and he says he uses it all the time for all his personal information.

I hand over the credit card that Josh had rushed to the hotel. When he first handed it to me, my fingers danced along my name *Joey Wilson*. It's a name I repeated so many times in the house because I only had ninety-days with it. The expiration date was set and it was a name that I'd never write or see in print.

Luckily for me, Josh changed all of that.

The clerk eyes me and I know she's putting the pieces together. I fiddle with my phone, looking disinterested, and wait for the receipt to print out.

"Sign here, Mrs. Wilson."

I smile kindly and sign my name. It's the first time I'm doing so and I hold the pen and paper slightly longer than necessary, trying to capture the moment. If I weren't in a dress store, I'd be taking a picture of this as a memory.

This new clerk comes around the front of the desk and hands me my dress. It's heavy, but going to be worth it.

"Thank you," I tell her. She smiles and wishes me good luck.

Good luck? Isn't that something you wish someone when they're trying to win a prize or a game? Wouldn't best wishes be better in my case?

I look over my shoulder at the lady who helped me, but she's deep in conversation with another bride-to-be. Apparently my status as Josh Wilson's wife doesn't mean much to her. I'm not naïve in how things work, but I do know she should be paying attention to me.

As soon as I step out of the store, there's a swarm of people that come rushing my way. In an instant, my heart is beating faster and my eyes are calculating the distance from where I am to my car. It's too far and I'll never make it in time.

My name is called out as I start down the street, but I ignore them. I'm pushed, shoved, and people step in front of me with flashing cameras and tape recorders. Questions are hurled at me from every direction.

"Joey, what you doing in Daphne?

"Did you and Josh move here?"

"When's the wedding?"

It's clear to me now why the sales agent didn't want to help me. Her conscious got the best of her after she alerted the media that Josh Wilson's wife was in her store buying a wedding dress.

I keep walking, pushing my way through the crowd until the questions change, and stop me cold in my tracks.

"How do you feel about Josh and Jules Maxwell having a baby?"

"Is the wedding on now that he knows about the baby?"

"Will you be a part of the baby's life?"

"Did you know she was pregnant when you said yes on the *Helen* show?"

I try not to let my steps falter when I hear the words "Jules, Josh, and baby" yet they do. I know it's caught on film and I'll be the laughing stock of all the celebrity news outlets, but I don't care. I cut behind another car and jaywalk across the street, running until I've reached my car. Inside, the tinted windows give a little reprieve, but not much. I bite the inside of my lip to keep from crying. I know not to trust everything the media says, but I knew, deep in my gut that we weren't done with Jules.

The reporters follow me to the hotel and park haphazardly in order to corner me again. I rush by them, praying that they won't follow me to my room. As soon as I see the security guard, I tell him that these people are bothering me, and he blocks their way into the lobby.

I take the stairs, but it won't be hard to figure out which room is ours. The hotel isn't that big and no one is going to expect Josh to be staying in a double. When I reach the third floor I'm out of breath and my arms hurt from carrying the dress.

The tears start to fall before I'm even at the door. I can't control the sob that takes over my body. I don't even have to find out if it's true or not, no one lies about being pregnant. The last question replays over and over in my mind. Either she was pregnant before Josh went on the show, or he cheated on me after. I don't want to believe that he cheated on me, but I can't help but think that he did especially after I left with Bronx.

As soon as I open the door, I stop dead in my tracks when Josh stands. Everything I've been told is true. He's home early and he's here to tell me that he's leaving me for Jules. They have the history and he and I don't. I can't compete with that.

Two things in his life that he never wanted are happening: he's married and he has a baby on the way. I knew in my heart never to bring up children because he made it clear that he didn't want to be a father. I accepted that. I knew that when I said yes to him. And because of a child I'm going to lose him.

Maybe he wasn't even mine to begin with and I was on borrowed time. It seems that my time with Josh Wilson has expired.

"You bought a dress?" He sounds shocked. His eyes move from the garment bag I'm holding to my watery eyes. "And you're crying."

I let out a sob and he comes to me, except I hold up my hand. I don't want him to touch me right now.

"Joey—"

I shake my head and find the courage to speak. "It seems

… I took your advice and left the hotel. I thought I'd check out a few of the shops on Main Street and found this wedding gown boutique, and after running the pros and cons of why you want a wedding through my mind I finally went inside. I fell in love with this dress," I take it and toss it on the counter, not caring if it gets ruined, "and the clerk recognized me. At first I thought she was sweet, but that sweetness quickly turned sour when she started to ignore me and the other clerk had to check me out. Seems like she had called the media, and when I stepped outside I was bombarded.

"I was handling it, keeping my head down and not showing them that they were getting to me until they dropped the most epic bomb ever."

He nods, because he knows what's coming.

"When were you going to tell me?"

"Today," he says, taking a step forward.

"That seems convenient since this is the first I've heard about it. I read the sites, Josh, no one has said a thing."

"I only found out today, Joey. You have to believe me." He takes my hand and I willingly follow him to the couch, but I put some space between us. His face falls when he sees me slide to the other end. He can't fix this with sex and sweet talk.

"Jules showed up right after you and I hung up. I didn't know what to think at first, and I still don't. I'm so confused."

"Is she pregnant?"

He nods.

"Did you cheat on me?"

Josh moves to the floor, getting down on his knees. He pushes himself between my legs and begs me to look at him. When I do, I see tears, torment, and fear etched across his beautiful face.

"I did not cheat on you. I haven't seen Jules since the end of the show, Joey, and I didn't sleep with her in the green room if that is what you're thinking. I love you, Joey. Not her.

You're the one I want to be with."

I shake my head and wipe angrily at my tears. "So she's really pregnant."

"Yes, she's showing. She said she's about six months or something."

"Great."

Rising, I go into the bedroom and shut the door. He follows, coming behind me to hold me. I let him, but don't return the affection.

"I'm scared," he says, breaking my heart into pieces. He doesn't want to be a father, but I know he will. And forever, as long as Josh and I are together, Jules will be there.

"What are you going to do, Josh?"

"We, what are *we* going to do," he counters.

I turn in his arms and see the agony he's going through. "*You.* I didn't get her pregnant. I didn't try to ruin her life on national television. I didn't try to ruin one of the happiest moments she was feeling by showing up and stealing you away. Jules is *your* problem, not mine."

"But you'd be the baby's step mom."

And that's when it hits me. I don't want that. I don't want to be second best in Josh's life or even an afterthought. Babies are hard work, and they need a lot of bonding. Jules will likely demand that Josh spend time at her place with the baby and I don't think I can live like that.

CHAPTER
ten

Josh

I've seen Joey cry, but not like this. Every few seconds there's another sob and there isn't shit I can do about it. Both our phones have been ringing off the hook and once we shut those off, the hotel phone started. I'm so fucking torn and confused. My wife is in agony and my ex-girlfriend is pregnant. If my life isn't a fucking soap opera, I don't know what it is.

All the curtains are drawn in our room and the lights are off, aside from the closet and bathroom light, with the only sounds in the room coming from Joey and my beating heart. The paparazzi are outside, setting up camp to make sure that we stay put. They want an exclusive. They want to be the ones to dig the knife deeper into Joey's chest the minute she walks out the door with questions about Jules. Staying here isn't an option, but switching isn't either. We're in a small town and people are going to find us no matter where we go now. The only phone call I've made is to Matt, letting him know the situation and to make sure the director knows I won't be in for a few days. Joey is far too important to me and right now this is where I need to be. If that means they have to put filming on a hiatus, then so be it.

My wife won't let me touch her and she doesn't want to talk. When I'm not sitting, I'm pacing the floor, begging Joey to listen to me, except I don't have anything to say. Every time I open my mouth, nothing comes out and I'm frozen. I've told her that I'm sorry, but it's not enough. And when she asks me what I'm going to do, I clam up. I don't have a choice and she knows this.

Being a father is something I never wanted and now it's being thrown in my face because I trusted the wrong person. If this were happening to Joey, I'd be fine with it, but not Jules. I'm in love with Joey and want to spend the rest of my life with her. With Jules being a part of that I'm not sure it's going to happen. Joey hates her, and with good measure. Hell, I'm starting to hate her. Jules is ruining my fucking life right now and I have no one to blame but myself.

"Where are you going?" I ask Joey as she stands up. Her back is to me, but I don't need to see her face to know what she looks like right now.

"I'm going to pack."

"Pack for what?" I walk over to her and see her shudder when I step behind her. My throat swells as tears threaten to fall.

"I'm going home."

"Your home is with me." My voice is barely audible when I say the words. If she leaves me, I won't know where she is. I don't know where our home is right now because living out of a hotel isn't a life that we should be living. I don't want her home to be in Springcreek, Oregon, but with me. *I* should be where home is, not where her parents live.

"This isn't a home, Josh."

"We'll go together."

She shakes her head and moves away from me, but I

follow. I'm not giving up without a fight. It's out of desperation that I grab and spin her around so she's facing me.

"Talk to me, damn it," I beg.

"What do you want me to say, Josh? Huh? Do you want me to tell you that everything is going to be okay and I'm happy to share my fucking Christmases with Jules and your child? That everything I envisioned for us, that I have been dreaming about these past few months will never happen because you'll be tied to her forever? If anyone should be giving you a child it should be me, but you made it very clear that you didn't want one and now you're having one with her," she cries out. "I can't do this, Josh. I just can't. You don't understand how she makes me feel. She's mean and vile, and in love with you. She's having your baby and that is something you and I will never share."

"So you're going to leave me?" I ask. My hands go slack on her arms, feeling defeated. She takes a step back and I feel our bond slipping away.

When she walks into the closet, she crumbles to her knees. The wedding dress she bought earlier hangs there. I made sure to hang it up so it didn't get ruined lying on the too small counter in the kitchen. I wanted her to buy a dress, commit to a date that we could get remarried and she did, for me, only for me to ruin it for her.

Getting down on my knees, I pull her into my arms. She comes willingly and cries into my shoulder. "I'm so sorry, Joey. Tell me what to do to fix this. Please. Please don't leave me," I say these words over and over as I rock us back and forth. Her tears wet my shirt and mine dampen her hair. I knew shit was too good to be true for us.

"There isn't anything you can do. You have to be in the baby's life. I can't ask you not to be, nor will I stop you."

"I will if that is what you need. You're my life, Joey." The words tumble out of my mouth before I realize what I'm saying. She glances at me briefly, then returns to my shoulder.

I saw the look in her eyes; she knows I was wrong for saying that. Being that parent would put me in the same category as my father, something I've strived to never be. He always chose his wives over me. And that is something I'll never do. Joey knows this and so do I.

We stay like this for hours, wrapped in each other's arms while sitting on the hard closet floor. Every part of my body aches, but none more so than my broken heart. Joey is the only one who can heal me, and deep down I know that's not going to happen. The wedding I want to give her, the traditional honeymoon and a life are slipping away faster than quicksand because of a foolish mistake I've made. Even as I sit here with my wife cradled to my chest, I'm asking myself when this happened and for the life of me I can't remember. I couldn't even tell you the last time I was with Jules before the show because I've been so consumed with Joey and the life we're trying to build that Jules was no longer a factor.

Well into the hours of the morning we finally move to the bed where I hold my wife to my chest and remind her how much I love her. The emotions we're both feeling are different. Joey's hurt, I'm scared. I'm scared of losing her over something I could've prevented, but was too stupid to pay attention to. Even though sleep evades me, I close my eyes and pray for some answers. Anything to guide me, tell me how I'm supposed to survive this with Joey by my side, plus raise a child with Jules. Joey's right, I'll be there for the baby because it's the right thing to do. No, it's not the right thing; it's the only thing to do. *I won't be like my parents* … but even as I say that in my head, I can't help but wonder, *do I put Joey in front of the baby or does the baby come first?*

Sometime by mid-afternoon there's a knock on our door. Neither of us moves because neither of us cares. As much as I want the knocking to stop, it doesn't, and once my name is called I know I have to get up and answer it. Thing is, I don't want to let go of Joey for fear that once I do I'll never get to hold her again.

She makes the decision for us by untangling herself from my arms and rushing toward the bathroom, leaving me no choice but to get up an answer the door.

"I'm coming," I yell out, hoping the knocking will stop. Through the peephole I see Matt standing there, looking like he's run a marathon.

"Hey," I say as I swing the door open. He smiles, but it's not what I'm used to. He's in work mode.

"You fucked up, huh?"

Matt has been my agent since I landed my first role. Over the years we've become friends, but sometimes he forgets that he works for me, it's not the other way around. I glare at him, letting him know that his question is out of line. I allow the door to slam and follow him into the room, pausing to close the door to the bedroom. I don't know what Joey is doing in there, but Matt doesn't need to see her if she's not presentable.

"I know you fired Jason, so I took the liberty of using a friend to draw up some papers."

"What kind of papers?" I ask, moving toward the table where Matt has dumped his briefcase.

"The first one is a paternity suit. You're demanding that Jules have a paternity test done within forty-eight hours to prove that the child is yours. The second is a non-disclosure that Jules will sign. We don't want her going to the tabloids, ever, about anything to do with you, the pregnancy, or the child if it turns out to be yours."

"Okay."

"This one," he pauses before handing it to me, "is for your wife to sign saying if she seeks a divorce under the current circumstances that she won't ask for financial restitution."

I don't even look it over before I'm ripping it in half.

"What are you doing?"

"If Joey leaves me, she can have it all. I won't give a shit at that point."

"Josh …" His tone is full of warning, but I don't care.

"Look, we can go after Jules, slap whatever we want on her, but Joey is off limits."

"You're making a mistake," he says, causing me to shrug.

"The way I see it, Matt, the mistake was made when I started dating Jules." I leave him standing there and retreat back to the bedroom where I find Joey on the phone. She looks at me before telling whoever is on the other line that she'll call them back later.

"Who was that?" I ask.

"Um … Bronx."

In an instant my level of anxiety skyrockets. I can feel my face turning red as anger boils within.

"You were talking to Bronx about our problems?" I can't help but seethe as I ask her that question.

She huffs, setting her phone down on the nightstand. "Our problems are public. It's not like I told him anything he doesn't already know."

"It's our business, Joey."

"And Jules made it public, Josh. She made it everyone's business that she's pregnant and has been for a while, and is just now getting around to tell you. Who the hell does that? How did she not know before you went on the show?"

"She says she tried to tell me after, but I walked out on her to find you, except you had left with Bronx."

"Bronx is my friend." She sighs, rubbing her head.

"I'm your husband."

"Josh, this isn't a tit for tat. I was talking to a friend because he called. He's concerned. He knows how I feel about Jules. And he knows her. He knows what she's capable of. He doesn't think the baby is yours and thinks you should get a paternity test before you commit to anything."

Bronx and I are not friends, and it makes matters worse

that Joey insists on keeping him in her life. I know they were friends before the show, but that doesn't help the situation. He had a thing for Jules and was the catalyst for breaking us up. I'll never look at him the same, or ever want to be friendly with him, but maybe he's right. Matt seems to think so as well.

"I know how you feel about her, too, Joey." I get down on my knees in front of her and take her hands in mine. My thumb moves over her engagement ring, the one I placed on her finger officially almost a month ago. "But I need you here, with me. I need you to help me figure this shit out because I'm scared as fuck to lose you."

Joey leans forward and kisses me, holding my face to hers. This is the first time I've been able to feel this way with her in over twenty-four hours and it feels like the first time we kissed on stage. Rising from my knees, I push her back onto the bed slightly and silently rejoice when she moves on her own accord. With my body hovering over hers, I lay down on her gently, relishing in the feel of her leg as it hitches over my hip.

"I love you, Joey, and nothing is going to change that," I whisper into her ear as I kiss down her neck.

"I'm scared."

I look into her eyes and see the unshed tears. My poor girl has cried so many tears in the last day that I didn't think she'd have any more. "I know. I am, too." I roll over onto my side and bring her with me, holding her leg as it drapes over my body.

"Matt is here. He has some papers for Jules to sign; one of them is ordering a paternity test. I think until we have the results we try to function as normal."

"It's going to be hard with the circus going on."

"I know, but we can't let them win. We can't let Jules think she's coming between us. Yesterday you found the dress of your dreams, let's set a date. We'll announce it and make sure we're only focusing on us."

"Okay," she says, nestling into my neck. "But, please promise me something?"

"Anything."

"That she never comes before me."

"I promise you on my life that she will never come before you." And that's a promise that I intend to keep. It doesn't take long for Joey to find some sleep, but even then the whimpers I hear from her continue to break my heart. I don't know how long I hold her before returning to Matt. I just know it wasn't long enough.

CHAPTER
eleven

Joey

"Hi Mom." I have avoided all her calls up until now. I don't know if it's because I have nothing to tell her or because I don't want her to think any less of Joshua. After taking a restless nap, Josh introduced me to Matt, his agent. I was leery at first, and then quickly realized that he has Josh's best interest at heart and I know Josh has mine.

"Please tell me it's not true."

Oh how I wish I could, but this is a crazy Hollywood movie playing out in real life. My life. I sigh deeply, saying nothing as I stare in the direction of Matt and Josh while they watch television and pick at the take-out Chinese Matt went and got for us.

"Oh, Joey." Her voice breaks and I find myself fighting back more tears. Just when I think I'm all cried out, more come, and at times I can't even stop them. I can't help but play ridiculous scenarios over in my head of what life is going to be like.

"I know, Mom." It's all I can say because there is nothing else. My mom saw the live footage of Jules during the show and she knows all about what transpired backstage. She knows everything about Josh because I was his ultimate fan girl and filled my mom in on their Josh and Jules relationship many times. Everything about my life right now is surreal and not in a good way. I can't tell if this is real or a nightmare—maybe it's a combination of both and I'm only waiting for the next fork in the road to determine the next scene.

"What's he going to do?"

That would be a loaded question to most people, but to me it's not. He's going to do the right thing because that's who he is on the inside. It's who I am. Does it hurt that I'm not the one giving him a child? Yeah it does, but this child shouldn't be held accountable because of Josh and Jules' actions.

"He's going to be a dad."

"And you?"

I glance over at Josh, who is watching me. "I'm going to be a step mom," I say, smiling at Josh. He leaves the table and comes over to me, kissing me on the side of my head and whispering thank you. It's not how I thought our life together would start out, but it's the course it's on now. The way I see it I have two options: support him and accept this fully or bail. I don't see leaving as an option.

After I hang up, I silence my phone, but Matt's continues to ring off the hook with people wanting to interview Josh and me. He declines for the both of us, telling the reporters that we're busy planning a wedding and that if they want the exclusive on that to send him a proposal. I know agencies pay big money to have exclusives, especially when it's a wedding, but never thought mine would be important to them.

It's when Jules calls that I find I can no longer breathe. Listening to her on speakerphone makes my blood pressure skyrocket and my heart race. I find that each time she says something my nails dig into the palms of my hand, but the pain isn't enough to make me stop. Josh paces as he listens to her and Matt converse, stopping next to me every so often to remind me that he loves me.

She wants to see Josh and talk, but is already putting stipulations on him. The first one being that I can't be there. I go to say something, but Matt holds up his hand, letting her finish her rant, and that's when I stop listening and retreat to the bedroom.

The door opens seconds after I close it and almost immediately Josh is pulling me toward the bathroom. He locks the door and turns on the shower, creating a sound barrier to prevent Matt and subsequently Jules from hearing us.

"Talk to me." He cups my cheeks with his hands, and when I look into his eyes I see the agony within him—it's stabbing me in the heart and ripping us both to shreds.

I shake my head. "I don't know what to say anymore."

"I won't go by myself. Matt knows this."

"He didn't tell her no," I point out.

"You and me, we're in this together … we do this as a team. So if she has to see me, which I'm not sure why she would need to, we go together."

I want to ask him what if I don't want to go? What if I want to stay as far away from her as possible? But I can't. His mistakes can't continue to haunt him. I've accepted it and need to support him.

He kisses me, and what starts off as sweet and tender turns frenzied. My hands fist in his shirt, pulling him as close as I can, but it's not enough. I'm not sure it'll ever be enough.

Pulling his shirt over his head, my lips roam over his broad shoulders, down to his defined chest and back to his neck. When I look into his eyes I see a hunger and know that it matches what I'm feeling. I give him a slight nod, letting him know that I want him, too.

Slow and methodical he takes off my shirt and removes

my bra with the flick of his wrist. His hands glide down my sides and he kneels until his lips brush against my belly.

"You should be the one carrying my child," he says before placing a kiss above my belly button. He has no idea what those words do to me on the inside. They rip and tear at what's left of my resolve.

Nimble fingers undo the button on my shorts and the sound of the zipper is lost among the booming echo of the water hitting the tub floor. Josh watches me as he tugs my shorts and panties down with one swift pull.

"This is not how I thought we'd be right now."

My hand brushes through his brown hair, the natural red highlights he has are muted from the poor lighting in the bathroom.

"As long as we're toget— ah oh God," I stammer out as his tongue swipes against my core.

"Fuck, Joey. I want to taste you, but I need to be inside of you." In a flash his shorts are down around his ankles and I'm on the counter. I watch as he slides into me slowly and his fingers dig into my hips as if he's afraid I'm going to disappear on him.

Everything about us right now is slow, methodical. Josh moves as if he's trying to memorize the way we feel together. Each thrust is proving a point.

"Josh." I need his attention to focus on me, on us, and not the drama surrounding our lives right now.

When he looks at me, the trance that he was in is broken. A wicked smile dances over his lips as he grips my hip to pound into me. I cry out, only for him to slam his mouth down onto mine and swallow each one thereafter.

His thumb works magic over my clit as my nails dig into his shoulder, leaving marks that are sure to piss off his production crew. Breaking away, I lean back, giving him a different angle that has me screaming out when he hits the place that I need him to be.

And now I'm looking at her, analyzing her with her perfectly manicured nails, styled hair, and cute as ever baby bump. I'm green with jealousy that it's her and not me.

"Doesn't matter. We need to talk."

He shakes his head. "I have nothing to say, Jules."

"Well I do." She looks at me and raises her eyebrow as if I'm in on some hidden secret with her. I stare back, trying to hold my resolve. "Do you mind?"

"Not at all," I say pointedly.

"Josh, tell her to leave. This is a private matter. As I told Matt on the phone, you and I will discuss everything to do with *our* child together. She's not to be involved."

Just this afternoon I told my mother I was ready to be a step mom, even when I'm not, but I was going to put forth my best effort because it would be supporting my husband. Now that I'm sitting here, listening to her, I want to scratch her eyes out and watch blood drip down her face while she cries to Josh about how mean I am. It would be comical, if I was a violent person, but I'm not. Even when I found Tony in bed with my best friend I just left. I was defeated and right now it's looking like I'm heading in the same direction.

"Joey is my wife and it's time you accept it. If we're going to co-parent, it will be the three of us. This isn't up for debate, Jules. You don't get to come in and interrupt my life because you lied to me. You're fucking lucky I don't sue you for fraud, and don't think that I'm not contemplating the idea. Everything you've done since I went on the show has been to undermine Joey and I've had enough."

"You were supposed to be with me, Josh. That show was fucking stupid, a joke. Well funny ha ha, it's over. Rob told me that you were getting an annulment and yet *she's* still here."

"Things changed in the house," Josh says, kissing me on the cheek. I can't help but smile, knowing full well that it's only adding fuel to the fire.

Jules throws her hands up in the air and looks at Matt.

"You told me she'd be gone by the morning. Make sure it happens."

By the time I realize what was said, the door slams and I'm being tossed onto the couch. I let out a scream when I hear the crunching of bones as Matt's head flies back and crashes into the wall.

CHAPTER
twelve

Josh

I react without thinking. The rage I feel is released in a crushing blow as my fist collides with Matt's face. His head pops back, slamming into the wall as Joey's deafening scream echoes in my ears. Blood gushes from his face and seeps through the gaps between his fingers as he holds his broken nose between his hands. I stand there with my chest heaving, waiting for him to do something in retaliation, but he doesn't. He looks at me, saying nothing.

"You. Work. For. Me!" I yell, enunciating each word so he understands what I'm saying. "What the fuck is wrong with you?"

"Just doing my job," he mumbles, adding more to my confusion. If I'm his job, why isn't he protecting me? Why isn't he protecting my wife?

Joey appears, pushing me out of the way so she can hand Matt some ice and a towel for his face. I shake my head, knowing that I've overstepped, but the more I think about it, the angrier I become.

"I'll do that," I tell Joey, moving her away from Matt. I don't want her cleaning up his mess or mine. It's bad enough she's involved in this shit. The white towel issued by the hotel turns red immediately, soaking through in no time.

"Do you want me to call housekeeping?" she asks. I shake my head; I can't trust them right now. "Maybe to get more towels."

She nods and rushes over to the phone while I head around the counter and grab the roll of paper towels.

"My wife shouldn't have to clean up your mess." I toss the roll at him, and he fumbles his catch but is able to hang on.

"You hit me!" His voice is hollow and that's likely because he can't breathe through his nose.

Leaning onto the table, I look him square in the eyes. "Start talking, Matt. I've already fired Jason, and as I see it, you're next. I won't put up with any bullshit. I'm so fucking done with all of this. How the fuck did Jules find out which room we are in?"

He looks from me to where Joey is talking on the phone and back to me. "I told Jules." Matt closes his eyes and acts like I'm about to hit him. I want to, but Joey wouldn't approve—although if she had heard what he just said, she may want to beat his ass herself.

"Why?"

Matt shakes his head, refusing to tell me.

"Get out. Take your shit with you."

"You need me."

I turn to face him. "What I need is for you to be my friend, to be on my side and not Jules'. What I need is for my agent to be there to make sure shit doesn't happen to my wife when I'm not around. Do you really think I can trust you? This was her safe place. The one place where no one could touch her and you let Jules know where we were. Get out, Matt. Your services are no longer needed."

Out of the corner of my eye I see Joey standing there,

watching everything go down. Matt packs his shit and leaves, cursing me every step he takes until the door shuts behind him.

Joey's arms come around my waist and I turn to face her. "I'm so sorry. I feel like I'm fucking everything up for you."

My hands caress her cheeks and I kiss her lightly. "It's not you, Joey. Jules has this way of worming her way into lives and once she's there, it's hard to get rid of her."

"This worries me, Josh. She's going around telling the important people in your life that you're the father of her baby. What if you're not? Have you considered that?"

I take a step back and let my hands drop. Jules likes to manipulate, but she's never lied to me. When I thought she cheated, Bronx confirmed that she didn't. It makes sense that this would be my baby.

"I don't think she'd lie to me about a baby."

"Why not?" Joey counters.

"Why would she? She already knows I'm not going back to her, so why bring an innocent life into this mess? Even if you and I were to divorce, I wasn't going back to her."

Joey shakes her head. "I don't know, Josh. A woman scorned and all that shit. She wants you back and what a better way to tie you to her than a baby. Bronx said—"

"I don't give a shit about what Bronx said. He's not my friend."

"He's mine, though, and he wants to see me happy."

"He kept you from me," I say, stepping forward. "He took you from me instead of asking me what was going on. There are no manners in Hollywood, he could've easily walked into that room and asked me, but he didn't. He played fucking hero and helped you hide. I looked everywhere for you, Joey. And he knew exactly where you were."

My hands go to my hair and pull in frustration. "Ugh," I yell as I kick the wall.

"Why can't you just accept the notion that this baby

might not be yours?"

"Because she wouldn't do that to me," I yell even though I don't mean to. Joey blanches at my words and steps away from me, moving into the bedroom and shutting the door. I know I should follow her, but I can't. Not right now. I need to think.

I pace the room, walking back and forth from the window and door. Deep in my heart I know Jules wouldn't lie about the baby, she knows how I feel. Even when we broke up, we stayed friends and hung out, which is probably what led to the situation we're in. It was always one too many drinks and we'd end up places I didn't want to go back to. The only time I stopped talking to her was when she was with Bronx and there's no possible way it's his baby. The odds are it's mine and I'm stuck no matter what.

When I finally cool down, I go to the bedroom only to find the door locked. I try the knob a few times, attempting to shake it loose, but it doesn't budge.

"Joey, open the door." My voice is as quiet as possible. The walls are paper-thin and we've already caused enough entertainment for the people next to us.

"Joey!" I jiggle the handle again, waiting for her to answer. The door remains locked and I can't hear her moving around on the other side. *What the hell is she doing?*

"Baby, come on, please open the door," I beg as I slide down the door, defeated. My elbow bangs against the door in a last ditch effort to get her to open up. I keep trying until the ache in my arm is too much to bear.

When I wake, my clothes are stacked on the table and the bedroom door is wide open. I rush in, looking for Joey, only to find that she's not there. I call out her name, but know in my heart she won't reply. Her missing suitcase confirms my worst fears, but still hanging in the closet is her wedding dress. The one she bought so we could have our dream wedding.

I search for my phone and find it sitting on my pile of clothes. Thankfully, it's charged and I dial her number immediately.

"Hello," she answers right off.

"Why did you leave me? You promised you wouldn't leave me, Joey. I wake up and you're gone."

"Josh, I'm doing laundry."

"What?" I ask as my chest heaves. I'm close to hyperventilating.

"Take a deep breath. I'm downstairs doing laundry."

I do as she says and try to labor my breathing.

"I thought it would be better if I did our laundry instead of sending it out. I don't really trust anyone right now."

"Oh God, babe. I thought you left me. I thought you gave up on me."

"I promised, remember?"

I sit and try to calm myself down. Tugging at the ends of my hair, I fight back the rush of tears. "Why'd you lock me out last night?"

She sighs and I can hear her moving around, hopefully to get some privacy. "I needed space, Josh. I think we're at an impasse where Bronx and Jules are concerned. I trust him, you trust her, and we don't trust either."

"He wants you, Joey, you're too blind to see it."

"Josh, he's happily married to Rebekah. She was there when we were talking. He's my friend and right now I need all the friends that I can get."

"I know. I'm so sorry that we're going through this."

"I know you are, Josh. We have to find a happy medium and deal with it."

"How long until you're done, baby? I really need to see you before I go to work."

Joey is moving again and the noise from the laundry room is getting louder.

"The timer is about to go off. I'll be up in a few minutes."

"I'll be waiting. I love you, Joey." I don't want for her to say it back before hanging up. I use the opportunity to jump in the shower quickly and wash off yesterday's events. The make-up artist is going to have a field day with the bags under my eyes.

By the time I'm out, Joey is walking in. As soon as she sets our clothes down I tackle her onto the bed.

"Josh, you're wet."

I shake my head, making sure she's getting the water droplets from my hair.

"Isn't that my line?" I ask, winking at her.

Rolling her eyes, Joey pushes me off of her. I don't go willingly, but move aside so she can sit up.

"Is that what you're wearing today?" She's dressed in sweats that are pulled up to her knees and a tank top. Her hair is piled high on her head with a crazy bun that makes her look taller.

"Excuse me?" she says, looking down at her clothes. "What's wrong with what I'm wearing?"

I stand and pull her to me. "You're going to work with me. I'm not risking anything. I don't want you here by yourself."

"I thought I wasn't allowed on set?"

Even though she put clothes out for me, I take what I need from the basket she brought up. "You're not, and if they want to fire me they can. I'm going to have the driver stop at the store for you to pick up some books or whatever and you can bring your laptop. My trailer is small, but you'll be on set and protected from the media."

"I need to change, give me a few minutes." Joey takes a pile of clothes and disappears into the bathroom. While she's changing I use the time to call the Blaze PR. They're a company I've used for public relations work and ask them to send someone out for me. They let me know that they'll send a contact over right away. I can't trust Matt, let alone use him to get my stuff done, so a PR company is my next best thing. Besides, they'll be able to issue press releases for Joey and I, saving us from interviews.

My next call is to the director, letting him know that Joey will be with me as it's a matter of security. He balks, but finally agrees considering we only have a few days left. It's not like she's going to watch filming; she'll be holed up in my stuffy trailer. It'll be boring as fuck for her, but at least she'll be there … for me. And finally to the hotel manager, asking him to make sure there is security downstairs for us.

When she comes out of the bathroom, my mouth falls open. Standing before me is my wife, who's completely changed the way she looked. Gone are the sweats—replaced with some stylish pants and a sleeveless shirt—and her hair is down and straight. Light make-up accents her tanned skin, making her picture perfect ready.

"Wow."

"Actor wife presentable?" She spins in a circle with me nodding the entire time.

"Let's go to work," I tell her, reaching for her hand. She stops and grabs her sunglasses, sliding those on as we leave the hotel. As soon as we exit the elevator I slip my sunglasses on as well and make sure she's right up tight to me.

"Mr. and Mrs. Wilson, I'm Johnny. Blaze PR asked me to step in until they can send someone to escort you for the remainder of your trip." Johnny shows me his police badge and all I can think is that Blaze doesn't fuck around when it comes to their clients. All I asked was for a rep, but some extra security works for me as well.

I shake hands with Johnny who is wearing a black suit that isn't shy about hiding the gun resting on his hip. I introduce him to Joey and he tells her that she'll be safe with him. This gives me a piece of mind, but she's still going to set with me. I'm not taking any chances even if the threat is Jules. I don't know how Matt is going to react after last night.

As soon as we step outside the noise level increases. Questions are screamed at us, some that I never want to hear again, and pictures are snapped. Not once did they ask us to look at them, just started slinging the dirt that will make me do more damage control. Even inside the car with tinted windows, they're yelling at us, hoping that we're actually going to answer them.

Pulling Joey to me, I kiss her forehead. "It won't be so bad once we go back to Los Angeles."

"That's good."

I pick up her hand and kiss her ring. "Maybe while I'm shooting today, you can look for a house, or condo? Something we can put a down payment on?"

She nods and smiles bigger than I've seen in the past twenty four hours, giving me hope that everything is going to be okay once we get back to our lives.

CHAPTER
thirteen

Joey

Los Angeles is where Josh is most alive. As soon as we left the airport, he started acting like a kid in the penny candy store. There's a different vibe to him now that we're back in his city and it makes me miss the early days that we spent in Alabama. He's talking a mile minute to his newly hired PR rep while I stare out the window at the scenery passing by, although it's not much to look at from the highway.

The last few days in Daphne were crazy to say the least. I couldn't go anywhere, not that I really wanted to, but once I was given a bodyguard it felt like my life was suddenly a cage. A matter of hours after the altercation with Matt, he decided that Josh was no longer a suitable client for him and filed a lawsuit against him for assault. That ignited yet another media storm and the prompt hiring of another lawyer to countersue. Except it's not Josh suing, it's both of us. I never knew you could sue for such trivial things, but according to Josh what Matt did was unethical and against his agent/client code—whatever that means. Either way, I've been told not to worry. But that's easier said than done.

It seems that our marriage is starting off very rocky. So far he's had to fire his lawyer because of me, and now there's the situation with his agent because of me. And I can't forget Jules. No, there will be no forgetting Jules, ever. I can't even count forward to eighteen years because she'll never be gone. In my mind Josh and I are married forever and the realization that our forever will include Jules truly sucks. They will always have a bond that Josh and I won't—and honestly, I'm not sure I can live with that. It's a hard pill to swallow, knowing your husband's ex is having his child and you're not. Even if I thought about broaching the subject of having a baby, I know deep in my heart he'll shoot the notion down. He doesn't want children. I knew this at the end of our ninety days and still chose to stay.

"What do you think?" Josh asks, his voice full of eagerness.

"I've been here before," I remind him with a smile that matches his.

"Yes, but now it's different. We're different." He squeezes my hand before leaning over to give me a kiss. He's right, we *are* different. When we left, everything seemed to be perfect. I was foolish to live inside a bubble thinking nothing bad was going to happen. I expected something from Jules, but in the way of tabloid fodder, a botched sex tape, or an exposé on how Josh broke her heart when he went on the show. Boy was I wrong on all accounts. Those I could've easily dealt with. I've watched enough Barbara Walters and TMZ to know what's real and what's not, to know when to laugh it all off and when to fan girl. Sadly, the fan girl in me is fizzling out because this Hollywood drama is too much to take.

We pull into an apartment complex that seems average. There's nothing striking about it, no security or high walled fence with a passcode keeping people who don't belong out.

When I look over at Josh, he seems excited and I want to ask him if we're picking someone up, except the driver has parked and is opening my door.

"We're home ... sort of," Josh says.

"Sort of?"

He shrugs. "Until we find our own place."

"Oh ..." Is all I can say as the driver reaches for my hand to help me out of the car. I let him because right now my legs are shaking and I need all the help I can get. Between the three of us we carry our bags past the people saying hi to Josh, up the flight of stairs, and down the open-aired hallway. The only thing preventing us from falling to our death—or at least saving us from being critically injured—is a wrought iron railing.

Josh opens the door, walking in first. I follow and the driver steps in behind me, hitting the back of my legs with the luggage he's carrying. He doesn't apologize or even say good-bye as he turns and leaves. The thought crosses my mind that I need to go with him because as I look around I'm having a hard time fathoming that Josh lives here. I know he said his place was small and affordable, but the living room is as big as the bathroom from the hotel we stayed at and that wasn't even a massive hotel.

"Welcome, home," Rob, Josh's best friend says as he comes out from what I'm assuming to be the kitchen area. I've seen him in many photos and a few interviews with Josh, but can't place which movies he's been in. He's good looking with his dark hair and defined cheekbones.

Josh and Rob hug, patting each other on their backs while I stand here. I feel like I'm intruding on some sort of bromance.

"You have to meet my Joey," Josh says to Rob as he turns to face me. I step forward with my hand out to shake his, but Rob pulls me into his arms, catching me off guard.

"You deserve a gold medal for putting up with him," he

remarks, holding on a little bit longer than necessary. He's right, I do, but not because of Josh as a person, but the drama that surrounds him.

"It wasn't so bad," I reply, referring to the show. Truth is, up until this past week, everything has been bliss.

Josh pushes Rob out of the way and takes me into his arms. I'm half expecting him to piss on me right in front of him to mark his territory.

"Let's get unpacked," Josh suggests, but refuses to let me go until Rob reaches for the bags that are on the floor. Josh follows with his arms full, leaving me nothing to carry and no choice but to follow them down a tiny hallway. I stand back when they enter what I'm assuming is Josh's bedroom and wait for Rob to exit. He winks at me when he passes by and starts whistling as he retreats down the hall.

"It's small," Josh says when I step into the room. I shut the door quietly behind me, wanting privacy. Small is an understatement, but I should've expected this. He warned me before that he lived simply because he was afraid to run out of money and yet we're looking at places to buy when maybe we should rent.

"It is, but it reminds me of my bedroom." As I look around I realize Josh and I aren't much different. Here I am, a college graduate who had to move home because her life went to hell in a hand basket right before her eyes and is living in her childhood bedroom. If we were at my house, Josh and I would be sleeping in a double bed, crammed into the corner with my embarrassing high school photos staring at us from the corkboard hanging on my wall.

He dumps the bags he's holding on his bed and hangs my wedding dress in his closet. Before I can blink, he's pulling me into his arms and kissing my neck.

"It's temporary. The first place we like, we move," he says in between kisses. I burn with desire for him, but quell any thoughts about being with him. I have a feeling we'll be regulated to the bathroom where the water can block out the noises that we make. It'll be like being back in the house with prying eyes and eavesdropping ears.

"Gah, you need to stop that," I tell him, pushing him away. The smirk across his face tells me that he has no intention of stopping. I shake my head and sidestep him so I can look around his room ... our room for the time being. There are scripts on his dresser and a small jewelry box. I'm tempted to open it and snoop, but I refrain. If there is something in there that he wants me to see, he'll show me.

A sudden burst of giddiness falls over me. I look at Josh, who is watching my every move.

"I'm in Josh Wilson's bedroom," I say, trying to contain my laughter.

"Seriously?"

I nod, biting my lower lip to hold back a squeal of delight.

Laughing, Josh scoops me up in his arms and lays us roughly onto his bed. "You're excited because you're in my room?"

"Yes. I can't explain it."

"After everything we've done, this box is what gets your heart racing?"

I turn slightly so I can see him clearly. He hasn't shaved in a few days and his eyes close as I run my fingers through his whiskers, loving the way they tickle my flesh.

"You make my heart race, Josh. Every time you're near, when you're close and when I know I'm about to see you again after a long day of being apart. You know how I feel and how being married to you has been like a dream, a surreal moment in my life and I'm often wondering if I'm going to wake and find that this isn't my reality. To me, you're a dream come true, my Prince Charming and my happily ever after. Our relationship is unconventional. We didn't date, you didn't have to woo me, and because of our circumstances I was pretty much a sure thing so yeah, being in your room, where you slept each night before you and I started sharing a bed, is a big thing for me. I can't tell you how many times I've imagined where you live or what your room looks like."

"You're such a little stalker," he says, tickling my side until I bat his hand away. Once my giggling fit subsides everything seems to shift.

"I can't wait to see your room, Joey. I want to go to your hometown, walk Main Street with you, share ice cream and sit on your back patio and drink a beer with your dad. I want to meet all your family, carry your cousins around on my back, and take a walk with you in the woods."

The way he talks about wanting to be at my house makes me question why we even flew to Los Angeles when we could've easily flown to Oregon. I want him to meet my family, be immersed in the love that we have for one another and cringe when my great aunt comes toward him to pinch his cheeks.

"So why are we here then?"

"I don't know. I don't start filming for another month and it's local. Let's go," he exclaims, jumping off of his bed. He picks up our suitcases from earlier and sets them on the bed. "Do we need to even unpack?"

Sitting up, I look at him questioningly. "We don't have tickets."

He shrugs. "So what? We'll go to the airport and buy them." Josh crawls over the bags and toward me until I'm leaning against the wall. His lips are soft and eager against mine. "Let's be spontaneous. I want to spend some time with your family before I have to start work again. I want to meet the people that created my wife and hear all about her childhood. Can we?"

Happy tears well in my eyes as I smile with an eager nod. "Yes, we can. My parents are going to be so happy."

Josh hops off the bed again, but this time he's pulling me with him. I laugh at how excited he is.

After Josh makes a phone call to get a car service, we grab our stuff and head back to the living room, where Rob is watching television.

"Hey, man, we're taking off to the beach for a bit," he tells him. The lie confuses me, but I play along.

"Yeah, man, I get it. You don't want me hearing you bang against the wall."

My cheeks flush red as Rob waggles his eyebrows at us.

"Something like that," Josh replies. I want to hit him but realize this is guy talk. They're best friends, not just roommates so they probably talk about crap like this. Girls do, too, believe me. If I still had my best friend I'd be gushing like a crazy fool about Josh.

Dread washes over me instantly when I think about her. Once she finds out we're in town, she'll be at my house wanting a piece of my happiness because taking Tony from me wasn't enough. My extreme upgrade in the man department will have her claws out, I'm sure.

CHAPTER
fourteen

Josh

I've never been one to be spontaneous, but listening to Joey tell me about how she feels being in my room sparked something deep within me. I know shit is about to get crazy with Jules and right now I want the solitude of family around me before my life becomes a media storm.

I missed the opportunity to meet her parents after the show's finale and owe it her and them to make this happen. I didn't even give Joey a chance to freshen up or decide what she wanted to take—I called for a car, picked up our already packed suitcase, and said farewell to Rob.

It's only after I bought our tickets and we're through security that Joey tells me there isn't a super easy way to get to her house. I mean, why would there be? Nothing since the show has been easy for us.

"Did you call and let your mother know?" I ask, as I'm loading the rental car with our luggage. This feels like déjà vu, except I'm not working and we're not hiding from anyone. I'm going to kick back and enjoy a beer or two with my father-in-law before life rears its ugly head at me.

"No, I thought we'd surprise them."

"What if they're busy?"

Joey furrows her brow, wrinkling her forehead. "Gross."

"Joey." My voice has a warning tone. "Have I not been keeping you well sated?"

"What?" She looks around to make sure no one is listening.

I go to her and wrap my arms around her shoulder, keeping her locked in my arms. "You're a dirty girl."

"You said it, not me!"

"Tsk, tsk. I was merely mentioning we should give them a heads up that we're coming. It would be the right thing to do."

She narrows her eyes at me, trying to figure out if I'm full of shit or not. After kissing her nose, I release her with a swat on her ass.

"Let's go, babe. Someone forgot to tell me that they live in the middle of nowhere and I'm ready to get sneaky with my wife in her childhood bedroom."

"Oh my God, Josh. Just drive!"

Unlike when we drove in Alabama, we don't stop in each little town that we came to. Joey suggested that we leave her parents early before going back to Los Angeles and maybe spend the night at the motels we came across and pretend like we're college kids on a budget. I laughed at the budget part because she still hasn't grasped the fact that I can afford nicer hotels. However, I agreed and told her that I'd thought it'd be romantic, which in turn she unknowingly batted her eyelashes at me.

It's the small things in life that I'm starting to hold onto longer, like when she's almost asleep and I tell her that I love her. Her reply is always the same, met with a sigh.

Between loud music, sign-offs, and all the munchies we could possibly eat we finally arrive at her parents. A long driveway that I never thought would end, opened up to this vast property with an amazing two story home complete with a wraparound porch. When I was little I'd see houses like this and wonder about the families who lived inside. And now I know.

Off to the left, in the distance, there's a pond with a dock. I don't remember Joey telling me anything about a swimming hole at her house, but then again I spent a lot of time trying not to get to know her. The yard is expansive and where the woods are close to the house, I see a trail starting. Hiking with Joey will be an experience I can't wait to embark on.

"You're the Waltons." I'm a little awestruck by their house. Someone is … well, was sitting on the swing, swaying back and forth until we pulled in and now they're walking down the steps toward us, one of whom happens to look like an older version of Joey. The screen door opens and I swear I can hear the faint squeak that I would expect the door to make as her father walks out.

Even before I see the inside, I know this is a home. This is where people are loved and they love the people who come to visit. I'm already imagining pictures of Joey all over the walls, and maybe even our wedding picture. It wasn't great, but it's still ours until we get a new one. It's been years since I've been in a home where two people love each other and I have a feeling I'm not going to want to leave.

"No, not the Waltons, only the Mitchells and now the Wilsons," she says. Joey gets out of the car before I can come up with a snappy retort. I watch as she runs to her parents who pick up their pace once they see it's her. This was a great idea … no, not great, freaking amazing.

My eyes are completely focused on what's happening in front of me. The love these two have for her, even though her mother signed her up for the show, is indescribable. It's only when her father starts walking toward the car do I get.

The man who is my father-in-law doesn't offer to shake

my hand. Instead, he pulls me into his arms and pats my back in a hug. And when he tries to let go I hang on a bit longer because it feels like I'm accepted. Hell, I can't remember the last time my dad hugged me.

"Nolan Mitchell," he says, extending his hand. "Our meeting is long overdue."

"Yes, sir, it is. I'm sorry it's taken me so long to bring her home, Mr. Mitchell."

He pats me on the shoulder and shakes his head. "Nolan. None of that Mr. Mitchell shit." Nolan chuckles and offers to help with our luggage.

I feel bad because we brought everything, which adds up to four suitcases and two carry-ons. We probably don't need this much, but I was in a hurry to get the hell out of there and spend some family time with my wife.

"Hey, babe." Joey steps to me when I reach her and her mother. Her hand rests gently on my stomach and she beams up at me. She's happy. I did this. I made her smile like this. "This is my mother, Ava. Mom, this is Josh." The way Joey says my name sends a jolt right to my groin. I bite the inside of my cheek, praying that the pain will counteract the stiffy that's forming. The last thing I want is for my mother-in-law to see my damn boner.

"It's a pleasure to meet you …"

"Ava. My son-in-law will call me Ava." She gives me a hug, but it's quick and when she's stepping away, I swear I catch her wiping a tear. "Come on, let's go inside."

Joey picks up one of the bags that I dropped and takes my hand with her free one. Side by side we walk up the steps and into her family home. The inside is decorated like one of those magazines you find at the doctor's office and I get the feeling that I'm not supposed to touch anything.

We follow her father down the hall and up a flight of stairs, down another hall and into her room. I know it's her room because it screams Joey. The walls are a light shade of pink, with posters of various celebrities, with me being one of them, hanging from them. Pictures of her friends, class ribbons, and other memorabilia adorn every space available.

"Make yourself at home. Beer's in the fridge when you're ready."

"Thanks, Daddy." Joey kisses him on the cheek and to my surprise he closes the door.

Setting the bags down near her closet, I look over everything while she sits on her bed. She doesn't tell me not to touch anything or come take things out of my hand.

"Who's this?" I ask as I pick up a framed photo and her face falls.

"Unfortunately, that's my two exes—best friend and fiancé—but in the middle is her brother. He died in a car accident and that's the only picture I have of him from when we were older."

If I were a lesser of a man I'd be pissed that she has a photo of her ex, but I'm not. I'm Joshua Wilson and this dumbass fucked up big time when he cheated on Joey. His loss is so my gain.

"Your room is cute."

"It's childish," she retorts.

I stalk toward her and push myself between her knees, falling into her until she's lying down. "It's you and I love it. I wish I could show you mine, but it doesn't exist."

Her fingers trace along my cheeks and jaw before moving into my hair. "We can make our own memories."

"I plan to, Joey. I want to make so many with you it's like my mind is a spinning Rolodex and stopping on what we're doing next."

"I'm so happy we decided to come here. I feel free. I can't explain it."

I crawl over her, pinning her with my legs. I don't think I'm going to be able to go a day without being with her and know we're going to have to get creative. I can't imagine she'll want to have sex with her parents here. Hell, she probably didn't want to have sex with Rob there, although I wouldn't have cared. It's definitely a guy thing.

"What are you doing?" she asks as I thrust my hips toward her.

"Your dad closed your door, that's like bro code."

"Bro code for what?" she asks, giggling.

"For having sex, Joey. Your dad gets it."

"Oh my God, Joshua." Her hands cover her face and I roll to my side, pulling her with me. "We can't have sex."

"Ever?"

When she doesn't answer I prod her some more. "Think about it, Joey. You're going to be sleeping next to me every night." My hand moves up and down her side. "You already know that I have the biggest hard-on in the morning. I mean, you've been taking care of it for me since I asked you to marry me again." I cup her breast, pulling at her nipple. "And I know how horny you get when you look at me, especially when you find me in bed ready."

Closing her eyes, she tries to ward off the ache she's feeling between her legs.

"My parents will hear us."

"Babe, we'll get creative and you'll have to be quiet, but I'm telling you right now, Joey Wilson, we'll be having sex."

When she slaps me on my chest, I use that to get her on top of me. Her eyes close again when she feels how hard I am. That's all it takes, me thinking about it and reminding her, to make me hard.

"Joey," her mom yells up the stairs, cock blocking me.

"Coming."

"No you're not, I didn't even get started yet!"

She covers her mouth and slaps me with her free hand. "You're going to be the death of me."

I sit us up and wrap her legs around my waist. Taking her face in my hands, I gaze into her eyes. "You own me heart and soul, Joey." I kiss her tenderly, letting my tongue trace the outside of her lip before seeking out the warm taste of her. She moves closer, adding friction to my erection and wrapping her arms around my neck to hold me in place.

"Joey!" her mom yells again, breaking us apart.

"Coming, Mom."

"Again with the lies," I mutter, shaking my head. I let her disengage from me and start picturing the grossest things I can, willing my hard-on to go away. The last thing I want is to go face her father like this.

"Are you ready?" she asks with her hand on the doorknob.

Nodding, I prepare to face my in-laws. I'm not stupid enough to know they won't ask questions, especially about Jules. Joey's already spoken to her mom about the situation, but I'm sure her father will have some sage advice. Hell, maybe he can tell me how to make Joey happy all while trying to raise another woman's child. I'm not sure the two go hand in hand considering Jules is on the warpath.

I already know Joey won't leave me because of the baby, she promised, but Jules and her antics are a different story. If Joey leaves me because of Jules, I'll never let Jules live it down.

CHAPTER
fifteen

Joey

My mom is running around, frantically making sure everything is perfect. It doesn't matter how many times I tell her things are fine, she's constantly trying to make them better in her eyes.

Josh and I have been at my parents' house now for a few days, and this by far has been the less stressful of our adventures. Even though the people in town know he's here, the sheriff has made it very clear that the media is not welcome. For Josh that's a relief. The last thing he wants to do is upset my parents, although when I saw my dad polishing his gun I don't think he would've been too upset.

Today is an impromptu wedding reception. I begged my mother not to throw a party, but Josh encouraged her and even sent out video invites of himself to all my family, which is the reason my mother is in such a panic.

Josh and my father are outside supervising the massive tent construction that will have a dance floor, white twinkling lights, and a DJ. I told Josh if we were doing all of this now, we wouldn't need to do it later.

"It's about the vows and declaring our love in front of our family," he said with a kiss on my nose. Since arriving here, he and my father have been as thick as thieves, staying up late tinkering in the garage, fishing in the early hours of the morning and napping in the recliners.

My parents are pulling out all the stops for this, and even though Josh offered to pay, they said they wanted to do this for us. Caterers have arrived and are setting up tables with an assortment of foods, veggies, and most importantly cake.

"I see you licking your lips," Josh whispers in my ear, pressing his chest to my back. I sag against him without taking my focus off the two-tier cake that sits not more than a few feet from me.

"It has buttery frosting."

"Hmm, maybe we should save an outside piece for later," he whispers into my ear. "I know a few places where I could lick some frosting off of you."

I squeeze his arms, hoping to convey that I'm game if he is. The last few days have been challenging. My bed is old and rickety, and even rolling over sounds like you're about to put dents into the wall, so sex on there has been out of the question. My parents never leave, therefore there is zero privacy in the house. The garage and the backseat of the car have been our preferred locations. We tried the woods, but I was afraid I'd get a critter in my cooter so I vetoed that idea.

"I almost wish we stayed in a hotel."

"Are you that horny, Joey?"

I nod, letting my head fall back into his shoulder.

"We just have to be more creative. I mean, we had sex in a house full of cameras. How hard could it be to hide from your parents?"

Turning in his arms, I raise an eyebrow at the smirk he's giving me. He thinks he's so damn smooth when in actuality he's not. Josh tells me all the time that I'm the one who has to be quiet, when in fact this man has the sexiest moans I have ever heard.

"You and my dad seem to be best friends, can't you convince him to take my mother out on a date?" I give Josh my best puppy dogs eyes while leaning into him. I even jut out my bottom lip for full effect. He tugs it with his teeth, making the growing ache inside of me stronger.

"All in due time, my sweet wife. Believe me, watching you strut around in your bikini has been no picnic for me either. The quickies aren't cutting it. My balls are turning as blue as that first condom we used."

I try to play it off, but I think he sees right through me. His eyes go wide while I look anywhere but at him.

"You," he says, almost seething yet he's still playful. "You lied to me."

"Not really."

Josh pulls me away from the hubbub that is surrounding us and into the woods, far from prying eyes and open ears.

"Admit it."

"Admit what?" I play stupid. I know full well what he's talking about.

"Tell me that we had sex."

"Duh." I can't contain my laughter. Josh closes his eyes as if he's trying to keep his temper in check.

"In the house, we were drinking and the next morning I woke up with a blue condom stuck to my leg. You and I had sex that night, didn't we? I've asked you this before, but you haven't come out and confirmed it. Why not?"

This time I look away. I remember the night clearly. Tequila did him in and he got frisky. I didn't stop him because I wanted it, wanted him. It was selfish of me, and when he didn't remember in the morning I thought it was easier to play it off than confirm we had sex. I didn't want to hear him say it was a mistake or that it should've never happened.

His fingers gently tug my chin, lifting it toward him. The

sincerity in his eyes makes my heart swim.

"Yes." The word is muttered and barely audible above the sounds of nature that surround us.

"Why didn't you tell me?"

"Because I didn't want to see the regret in your eyes, or hear that being with me was as mistake."

"I wouldn't—"

"You would've. You reminded me daily that we weren't going to consummate our marriage ... that after the ninety days was up, we were going our separate ways. I took advantage of you and didn't want to suffer the consequences. I figured if you knew, you'd hate me."

"I hated that I didn't remember, Joey." He cups my face with his hand, his fingers pushing into my hair to hold me. "I was only fooling myself when I told you we couldn't be together and hated that you listened to me. You kept your distance when I pulled you to me. Each time you backed away, I had to move next to you. Until I met you I didn't believe in soul mates or love, but you walked into my life and shocked the shit out of me. Now I can't picture my crazy, dysfunctional life without you."

"I could never picture my life with you. I felt cheated that we were matched on the show because look at me—"

"Babe, I look at you all damn day long and believe me, I'm not the only one. You're so fucking sexy, gorgeous, and smart and mine. All fucking mine."

He doesn't wait for a response, pulling me forward until our lips are crashing together. Our tongues touch, sending the most wonderful feeling through my body. I never want this feeling to go away. I crave it. I crave him.

My hands tug at his shirt, moving until I can feel his skin against my hands. My fingers roam over the planes of his abs and down around his back until they're pushing into the waistband of his shorts. Josh bends slightly before rising, making sure I can feel his erection growing. I have to touch him. I have to taste him.

Dropping to my knees, I work the zipper of his shorts to free his cock. He hisses and dives his hand into my hair after the first swipe of my tongue. Taking him into my mouth, I look up to see the hunger in his eyes. With his free hand, he's caressing my face and each push and pull into my mouth causes his eyes to flutter.

"Joey." My name falls from his lips in a hushed sound. He's trying to keep our activities on the down low from my parents and the unsuspecting guests that are starting to arrive. I block out their voices and concentrate on my husband. Josh undoes his shorts and widens his stance to keep his pants up, but to give me better access.

"I can't …" he says, pulling me up by my arms, forcing me to let go.

Wiping my mouth with the back of my hand, I wonder why he's made me stop.

"Go to that tree and face it." He nods at a tree, any tree, really.

I do as he commands and can see people mingling with my parents in their backyard. They're here for Josh and me, and we're too busy fucking in the woods to be with them.

Josh comes behind me and swats my ass. I let out a little yelp and he leans forward, reminding me to be quiet. His hands ghost down my sides, causing goose bumps to rise and a small chill to take over my body even though I'm heated. The button on my shorts is undone. Josh pulls my shorts down, painstakingly slow, letting the warm air coat my skin.

"Hold on, baby. It's going to be fast and hard. My cock is dripping and my balls are about to burst."

He wasn't lying.

By the time we make our appearance the yard is filling up. My mom eyes me warily and brushes some bark off my shoulder. As soon as my aunts, cousins, and every other female member of my family and friends sees Josh, I'm no longer visible. It doesn't matter that he's holding my hand, or kissing me on my temple—these women are focused on him and only him. I could be standing here naked and they'd not see me. And the best part about it, all I have to do is tell Josh I need something and we're moving on.

My parents dote on Josh all day, introducing him as their son and not son-in-law. My father says it with pride while my mother gushes on how she set us up. She wishes. As I sit now, watching Josh with my dad and the other men here, I see how much he has longed for a normal family. If normal is what we are. I mean, my mother did sign me up to be on a reality show where I had to marry a stranger.

Josh comes to me, kissing me on the cheek. "Have you seen the present table?"

I can't help but laugh because he's like a kid in this aspect. "I have."

"Who gets to open them?"

"We do, tonight after everyone leaves."

Pouting, he nuzzles into my neck. "Why do we have to wait?"

"Because it's rude to open a present at a reception. What if we already have the item, or don't like what they chose for us?"

Josh sits back up and implores me to look at him. When I do, he has a "are you kidding me" expression on his face.

"What?"

"We have nothing. We're guaranteed to love everything."

Shaking my head, I wonder how men survive in this world. "Would you like me to tell everyone that you live cheaply and ruin the Hollywood stigma that we all have where everyone lives in luxury?"

He looks around the yard for a few seconds before shaking his head. "Better not. Your dad might think I can't take care of you." Josh places his arm around me, using his hand to bring me closer to him. There are only a few instances when I appreciate this more than ever and this is one of them, because walking into the backyard is none other than my former best friend—the one who was to be my maid of honor, but decided screwing my fiancé was more important—and the dirt bag himself, Tony.

"What the fuck is he doing here?" Josh blurts out.

I glance at him, wondering how he remembers what Tony and Erin look like. He's seen one picture of us when we were younger.

"What?"

"Did you invite him?" Josh points toward the house and my mouth drops open. Standing there with gift in one hand and holding his wife's with the other is Bronx. And my mother is gushing over him.

"Well this just got interesting."

CHAPTER
sixteen

Josh

There are a lot of things I can take in life, but Bronx Taylor showing up at *my* reception at *my* in-laws' house is too much to take. At one time in our lives we got along. We are competitive actors vying for the same roles. I used to consider him a friend, not in the sense that we were hanging out, but in the way where we'd grab a beer after an audition or chat when we ran into each other … until Jules got in the middle. I blame her, mostly, but his quickly earned reputation of sleeping with casting directors, producers, and directors didn't help his cause. Once he set his eyes on Jules, our so-called friendship went downhill fast.

That's when I learned that having friends in this business was tricky. Sure I trust Rob, but that doesn't mean I'm divulging my secrets to him. I keep a lot of my shit bottled up because I don't want him slipping up one night or using something I tell him to his advantage. Not that I think he would, but it's better safe than sorry.

When Bronx entered the house and Joey went all

googly-eyed, I started to think she was nothing more than a fan girl gone crazy and wondered if I should second-guess everything, but when he spoke to her that wonderment turned to pure jealousy. They knew each other and it seemed better than Joey and I knew each other. I hated that. Still do. To make matters worse, he fucking stole her from me after the show. He knew damn well that all he had to do was open the door and I would've come out, but he just had to play the hero.

My blood boils as he and Rebekah talk to my in-laws. The way Ava puts her hand on his arm and throws her head back and laughs does nothing to calm me. I down the rest of my beer and mutter some obscenities meant for only Joey to hear, except when I look at her for a reaction—something from her to tell me I'm overreacting—I see her eyes are focused elsewhere. I try to follow her gaze, looking in the general direction as to what has my wife so upset, and that is when I see *him*. The man I want to thank for being so fucking stupid as to cheat on Joey so I could have her. He's getting a damn pat on the back for being a spineless piece of shit.

Another glance at Joey shows me that she's equal parts angry and upset and that's something I can't tolerate. This is supposed to be a happy day for her, not one filled with drama and bullshit from exes.

"Hey," I say, trying to get her attention. When she turns her head to look at me, it's her eyes that tell me she's about to fall apart and it's because of my sexual prowess. I do what any self-preserving man would do and kiss her. It's not chaste by any means. I make sure the onlookers see me putting my tongue in her mouth so they know she's fucking mine.

"What was that for?" she asks, breathlessly and with fluttering eyes.

"One: I don't need an excuse to kiss my wife. Two: because you're beautiful. Three: because I fucking love you."

"Is there a four, five, and six?"

"Are you being greedy?"

"Yes, because I'm freaking out on the inside. I'm afraid that my fairytale is turning into a nightmare and you're going to vanish into the house with that wench over there."

She says nothing about her ex, only her former best friend. Joey trusted her and her friend committed the worst possible betrayal. Taking her face between my hands, I make her focus on me.

"There isn't a woman in this world that can make me leave you, Joey."

"Even Jules?" she asks, catching me off guard. I thought I had squashed everything she's been feeling about Jules, but apparently not. Maybe those thoughts will never go away. Sort of like mine where Bronx is concerned.

"Especially Jules. What can I do to show you that I'm not going anywhere?"

"I don't know, Josh. Every time I think things are the way they should be, shit like this happens. My ex is standing over there like he was invited and he brought *her* with him."

"How do you think I feel with Bronx here?"

"I know," she sighs. "We should go over and say hi."

"To which evil?"

She shrugs. "I'll say hi to Bronx and Rebekah, you go over to Tony and Erin."

"Can I punch him?"

"Yep," she replies, standing. I know she's putting on a brave front for everyone when she really wants to go inside and hide. I don't blame her because that is what I want to do right now. Instead of going toward her ex, I take her hand in mine and follow her to our former roommates. I'm promising myself that I'm going to be nice.

Bronx is the first to extend his hand toward me. I do the right thing and shake it, gripping it hard enough that he knows I won't take any of his bullshit. I figure that while I can bury the hatchet, so to speak, for the day and let him enjoy the party, he still needs to know that he's not going to get a chance to eat my cake.

"You guys, I'm so happy you're here." Joey hugs Rebekah first, making me happy that Bronx wasn't her first choice. Maybe I'm worrying for nothing.

"When we heard about the party we couldn't resist," Bronx says, pulling my wife into his arms. Okay it's a hug, but still …

"Thanks for coming," I add, trying to be pleasant. "You look lovely as ever, Rebekah."

"Thank you, Josh. I'm enjoying married life, that's for sure."

Bronx smirks and I imagine it's what I do as well when I hear Joey say the same thing. Knowing your spouse is going to bed with you every night is definitely a perk of being married. That and I get to wake-up every morning with her in my arms.

"Are you going to say hi to Tony and Erin?" Ava asks Joey, who shakes her head. I don't want Joey to feel uncomfortable at our party, but I also don't want these bastards to know they got the best of her.

Or maybe she's not over him?

Nah, I don't believe that for a second. She's made it very clear how she feels about cheaters, and I know she worries about that when it comes to Jules. I wish I knew what I could do to make her understand that she owns me heart and soul and I'm not interested in Jules, even with the baby. Jules isn't who I want to be with—Joey is.

Taking her hand in mine, I walk us over to the people who shattered my wife's world. The woman's face lights up as if this is her dream come true. Too bad I'm going to be a fucking dick.

"Josh, what are you doing?"

Her hand goes rigid in mine so I tighten my grip. Joey has to know I'm not going to do anything to hurt her. Embarrass her, maybe, but it'll be worth it.

"You must be Tony," I say, standing in front of him.

He smiles. It's cocky and pisses me off. "I am."

"Right. Thanks for screwing her best friend so I could have her. Best fucking thing that's ever happened to me."

I don't bother introducing myself. Everyone knows who I am and if he doesn't then he's been living under a rock. Joey's and my love affair played out on national television and I honestly think that is the only reason they showed up here. They don't care about her happiness, just that she's married to me.

Joey doesn't have a chance to respond and neither do Tony and the former bestie. I take her away, back to where we were sitting, only to have my steps falter when I see Bronx and Rebekah sitting near our chairs.

"I love you, Josh."

Stopping midway, I pull her into my arms and subsequently my lips. Our family around us hoots and holler, making me smile against her lips. "I meant what I said. You're the best thing that has ever happened to me."

As soon as we reach Bronx, he's giving me a high five. "I never liked that douche in college."

That makes two of us.

"You guys are so cute," Rebekah says, making us all laugh.

I figure that maybe hanging with Bronx and Rebekah won't be so bad.

When Rebekah suggests we play Corn Hole, all I can remember is the day we sumo wrestled and she did some flying kick at my Joey. I think she scared the whole house with that ninja shit. But Joey wants to play, so we do. Others join in and before we know it we have a massive game going on. The best part, Joey isn't watching for her ex and when they leave, no one cares to notice.

"Time to cut the cake," Ava announces, much to the delight of the little kids that are here. I feel their pain; I've been waiting for hours while it's mocked me with thoughts of spreading the frosting all over Joey's body and licking it off.

Someone yells out speech and I look around, wondering who would even begin to say something about us. I could, but I'm a sappy bastard when it comes to Joey and I don't want my words to end up on TMZ by the end of the night.

"I'll say something." Bronx steps up to the table, standing in front of us and holding a glass of champagne high in the air. "I think I'm the only one here who knows both Josh and Joey. It's easy for me to say that they look happy, and it is because I've seen them both when they've been down. It's clear to see that they make each other very happy, and while it may be a little sickening to see them giddy and in love, I wish both my friends a very happily ever after and want them both to know that whatever lies in their path, their love for each other will prevail. Here's to Josh and Joey Wilson."

Everyone says, "Hear, hear," and starts chanting kiss so I do and kiss Joey as tenderly as possible. I can't imagine a day when I don't want to kiss her and hope that I never experience it. I have to admit that his speech was very nice when he could've slayed me. Maybe I'm not giving him enough credit and I can hopefully put my feelings aside for the friendship that he and Joey share.

"Stop that and cut the cake," her mom chastises us. I pull away, but keep my hand on her neck with my thumb stroking her cheek softly. "I swear you two never stop touching each other."

Her mother has no idea how bad I'm craving to be pressed against her body, to have my wife writhing in ecstasy underneath me, to have her ride me so I can see firsthand the pleasure she's experiencing. As much as I love being here, a hotel would've been better for us. Or a tent, camper, anything where a bit of privacy is afforded so I can hear Joey scream out my name as she comes.

The knife is handed to the both of us and as we grip the handle we move slowly toward the cake. This is a symbolic moment in our marriage—who cares if it's coming months after we tied the knot. One of the caterers appears behind us after we make the cut and gives us each a half of the piece of white cake.

Joey and I inch closer together, and a smile spreads across my face as we reach each other's mouth with our slivers of cake. As soon as I feel the moist cake with buttery frosting hit my tongue, I know she's not going to smash it into my face. I take it all, making sure to suck her fingers into my mouth, and when she does the same to me, my cock jumps to attention. Joey's in my arms with her mouth pressed to mine. I clamp my mouth shut, fearful that she's trying to steal my cake.

Everyone around us starts to clap and I can't help but smile against her lips. "Are you happy, Mrs. Wilson?"

"Immensely."

"Me too."

Joey and I return to mingling with the guests and apparently now is the time for pictures. We pose with everyone and never alone. I refuse to remove my arm from her shoulder, even as my phone continues to vibrate in my back pocket. All day, Jules and Matt have been calling me and I've let them all go to voicemail and refuse to answer any of my text messages. Until I met Joey I was attached to that thing, but since her, since we got out of the house, she's the only one I care about talking to. She's the only one I need.

CHAPTER
seventeen

Joey

Leaving my parents was hard, but coming back to Los Angeles is almost refreshing. As much as I love being home, the thought of making a new home with Josh is exciting. I'm ready for this new adventure.

He has one week before he begins filming his next movie, leaving us barely any time to find a place to live. Instead of going back to his apartment with Rob, we checked into a hotel where he proceeded to make me scream his name over and over again until even he couldn't move. I was never this sexual with Tony and maybe that's why he sought attention from someone else. With Josh, everything seems to click. We aren't fumbling around and touching each other awkwardly. It's natural and the responses we get from each other are automatic.

Today, we're driving around, looking at everything from an apartment in a hotel, to houses and condos. Nothing has jumped out at us yet. The apartment and condos are nice because there isn't any yard maintenance, but I want to feel my toes in the grass on a warm spring morning and plant some flowers. And I'm thinking of the future. There's a baby coming and he or she will need a place to play, assuming Jules lets Josh parent in our home. Deep down I know it's going to be a battle, and while he deserves equal custody, sometimes I wonder if Jules isn't planning to make this extremely hard on him.

Before our reception ended, Bronx pulled me aside and spoke his mind again, telling me that he doesn't think Josh is the father of Jules' baby. I thought about bringing it up to Josh again, asking about the paternity test, but didn't want to ruin our vacation. Now that we're back in L.A., though, I'll speak my mind more. This is my life that she's messing with, too.

"This is the last house on the list," Josh says, following our real estate agent through a gated community. The homes are all single-family with front yards, sidewalks, and charm.

"These houses look nice."

"The one we're seeing is brand new."

I continue to look out the window at the people washing their cars; little kids riding bikes and jump roping.

"The house is fairly new, but it might be out of our price range."

"What neighborhood is it in?"

"Beverly Hills. We're on Mulholland Drive, you've heard of this road, right?"

I nod and continue to gaze out the window as we drive up the road. The higher we get, the better the view and the bigger the houses.

"Josh, these houses …" My breath catches when our relator comes to a stop in front of a single level gray home.

Josh comes around and helps me out of the car and we meet our agent halfway up the driveway. I notice the garage first; it's mirrored glass reflecting back on us. I've never seen anything like it. The walkway is slate and leads to a frosted glass door. I hesitate before I walk in, already aware that I'm in love with the house and I haven't even seen it, and knowing that Josh is already worried about the price because of the location.

"Oh my God," I gasp as I step inside. Everything is white, gray, and black with the perfect accent of brown for hardwood floors. The agent drones on about the specifics of the house, but my eyes are focused on the glass walls which the agent is opening as we walk through. Josh takes my hand and leads me through the massive rooms, but I'm lost in a daze, imagining myself living here.

A small wall with a fireplace separates the living room and dining room, making it visible from both sides, and off the living room is the master bedroom. When we step into the master, the wall of windows slides open, revealing the same view from the other rooms.

"Holy shit," I murmur, stepping out. The large patio and outside kitchen is nothing compared to the pool. Josh chuckles behind me before dragging me into the master bath, walk-in closet, and exercise room. "I'd never have to leave."

"I'd be okay with that," he whispers into my ear.

We look at the other two bedrooms, which have their own bathroom and a walk-in closet.

"This house is massive," he says.

"This house is beautiful," I counter, knowing it's only a dream. We could never afford it.

The fourth bedroom is smaller, but still has its own private bathroom. I already start thinking about nursery decorations and a pang of jealousy hits me square in the chest. This isn't my baby, but we're looking at houses so that he or she can live with us, when I want to be looking because we're having a baby and need the space. The rest of the house consists of an office, breakfast nook, and kitchen. The color scheme is carried throughout the house for complete flow.

Josh takes me outside to the terrace. "What do you think?" he asks, while holding me.

I shake my head. "I love it, but it's too much."

"Can you see yourself happy here?"

"I'm happy wherever you are, Josh. We've seen some great places today that are affordable, smaller. This is too much house for the three of us." I smile, but it's weak. I'm trying to include his child with Jules in our decision because as much as I want that part of my life to go away, it's not happening anytime soon.

"What if there were four of us, or maybe five?"

I look at him questioningly. "What are you talking about?"

Taking my face in his hands, Josh kisses me softly. "After being with your family I want that. I want it all, Joey. Watching your cousins run around and jump in the pond and seeing your parents dote on them, I want that for us. I want to have children with you."

"What?" My eyebrows rise as I step back. "Is this because of Jules?"

"God no. This is because I saw what a real family could be like and I know together we can do that."

"Wow."

"Do you not want kids? I thought—"

I hold my hand up to stop him. "I do. I always have. I knew with you it'd be a hard sell, but when Jules told you she's pregnant I thought that would make you shut down completely. That children would never be an option for us."

"I'm making it an option if you want, Joey." He pulls me back into his arms.

"Okay."

"Yeah?"

I nod and wipe away the tears that have fallen. "Yeah."

"Perfect. Now before we decide about the house, let me tell you that it comes fully furnished if we want and the owner has never lived here."

"What does that have to do with anything?"

"It means we get to be the first ones to have sex in the house!"

I roll my eyes. "Is that all you think about?"

He smiles then laughs. "You know, apparently it is. I can't get enough of you."

I want to tell him that I feel the same way, but I like the idea of him needing me. He can have anyone he wants and he's chosen me and it's not because of circumstance. And I still fear he could leave me for Jules. They have history and the baby is coming sooner rather than later. Does that mean I go off the pill now to secure him, or do I trust that he's not going anywhere?

"What do you think of the house, Mr. Wilson?" the agent asks Josh, knowing full well he's the one with the money.

"We love it."

"Would you like to make an offer on it?"

Josh looks at me for an answer, but I can't give him one. Can I see myself living here? Yes, I can. I can see it all. My parents visiting, my cousins doing cannon balls into the pool, Josh over by the grill and our children being held and loved by our family.

"Yeah," he answers, never taking his eyes off of me. "All cash offer. I want to close tonight if possible."

"I'll be right back, Mr. Wilson."

"Josh—"

He silences me with his lips. "I saw it, too, Joey and I want it. I want the noise from our visitors, the wet feet traipsing through the house. I want the sounds of laughter and the smell of a home to be all around us, and this house does it for us."

"But it's expensive."

"It's what I'm making off my next movie. We'll be fine. I promise."

We sit on the edge of the pool with our feet in the water. Josh says the house is ours unless someone else is coming in higher, but cash usually speaks louder.

"Do you like the furniture?"

"I wouldn't change it now, if that's what you're asking. This house is huge, Josh. I don't know where I'd begin if I had to decorate it myself."

"Mr. Wilson?"

"Yes," he replies, glancing over his shoulder.

"The house is yours. My assistant is bringing the paperwork up now. She'll be here in an hour. Here are your keys." She drops two sets of keys into his hand and disappears.

"Open your hand." I do and he closes it as soon as the keys are set in my palm.

"Welcome home, Joey."

I can't help but smile as I look over my shoulder. The house is still open and I see right into our bedroom. The navy blue comforter is inviting and I know that tonight I'll be in that bed with my husband.

As soon as the papers are signed, we head back to the hotel and pack our things. Now that we have a place, my mom will be able to ship the rest of my clothes to me and a few of my personal belongings that I left behind when we returned to Los Angeles.

Our next stop is Josh's apartment. He's not sure how Rob is going to take the news, but figures that he has to realize Josh and I can't live there with him. I'm not going to lie, but moving to a house with twenty-four-hour security is very welcomed. I hate that anyone can have access to Josh whenever they want.

Rob's watching television when we enter and Jules is sitting next to him. Or she was until the door opened and she put some space between them. Josh glances at me and shakes his head. I can see the anger in his eyes, but can't tell if it's because Jules is here, or if it's because her and Rob were sitting so close to each other.

Either way, he doesn't say anything and pulls me down the hall into his room where he starts emptying his dresser onto his bed.

"There are black bags under the sink … I think. Can you go get them?"

"You want me to go out there?" I point toward the living room where my worst enemy is sitting.

"If I go, she'll talk to me."

"If I go, she'll say nasty shit to me and I might hit her."

A smile spreads across his face before he realizes that he's laughing and shouldn't.

"So what do I do?"

The only bag in his room large enough to hold his clothes is my wedding dress and I don't want him to see it, so taking it out of the bag isn't an option.

"Come back tomorrow and pack?"

"Yeah, that's a good idea," he says.

Before we leave, though, I snag my dress out of his closet and drape the garment bag over my arm. If Jules is here, I'm not leaving my dress.

"I'll carry that for you." Josh slings the bag over his shoulder and walks out of his room, letting me shut the door behind him.

"Joshie, we need to talk about the baby."

He pauses near the door. I make sure to hold his hand so he knows that I'm there for him, and so she sees that we're together.

"Not today, Jules."

"When? Because every time I call you, you don't answer."

"That's because I don't want to talk to you."

She points to her stomach and mine rolls. "This is happening whether you accept it or not."

"I'm aware."

"So talk to me then. We're going to be a family, Josh." She

tries to touch him, but he steps back.

"That's where you're wrong, Jules. Joey is my family. You and I will co-parent, but when it comes to family photos, you'll be nowhere near ours."

"And neither will she." She points at me, her voice rising high enough to get Rob to stand. "This is our child, not hers, and I won't let the harlot who stole you away from me be a part of our baby's life."

Josh groans and has to let go of my hand to run it through his hair. "She's not a harlot, she's my wife."

"You cheated on me with her. That makes her a harlot in my book."

"Well your book is skewed, Jules. We were broken up long before I went on the show," he fires back, but it does nothing to curb her anger.

"I'll make you pay, Josh."

"I have no doubt, Jules. I have no doubt."

Josh motions for us to leave so he doesn't have to listen to her anymore. Once inside the car he doesn't say anything as we drive back to our house. Pulling into the driveway, he hits the garage door opener that he put on his visor earlier.

"We're home," I say, trying to ease the tension.

"Yep. Come on, wife, we have a lot of rooms to christen. And I think we should start in the pool."

He doesn't give me a chance to protest. By the time we get through the mudroom clothes are already being shed.

CHAPTER
eighteen

Josh

There's one day until I have to get on set and I'm already dreading it. I wish I hadn't signed onto the movie, but it was done a year ago, long before I met Joey. The only saving grace is that we're shooting on the lot and that means I'll be home each night with her. Breakfast, too, unless it's an early shoot.

Much to my dismay, I'm meeting Barry for coffee this morning. I asked Joey if she wanted to come, but she opted to lounge by the pool and bask in the sun. To say she loves our house would be an understatement. I know I fucking love it and am pretty sure Joey's sentiment is right up there with mine.

The coffee shop is buzzing when I walk in and it takes me a minute to spot Barry. I don't usually conduct business in public, but considering my agent and I aren't on speaking terms right now this was better than inviting Barry over to our house. He's already asked Joey and me to do another reality show, but she's declined and I respect her decision for that.

"Morning, Josh."

"Barry." I pull my chair out and sit down across from him. It's only a matter of seconds before a waitress is taking my order.

"How's married life?"

"It's pretty damn awesome."

He chuckles as if there is something funny about being married. I should Google him and see how many times he's been married or if he's a perpetual bachelor. A quick glance at his hand shows no ring, or ring line, so I'm guessing he thinks he's a playboy. Barry's an old man with a rounded belly and balding head, but with a fat checkbook. He's every starving actress's knight in shining armor.

"Given any thought to my proposal?"

I take a sip of my coffee, letting the hot liquid heat my already warm body. I don't know why I don't switch to iced coffee. It seems smarter to drink when living in California.

"Joey's not on board."

"We can film you."

"Seems pointless, don't you think? Who the hell is going to want to watch a show about me?"

Barry leans forward. "You and Jules. I've already spoken to her and she's ready to sign on the dotted line. I'm sure if you tell Joey that you're going to do a show with Jules, she'll jump on board."

"Or she'll cut my dick off. Don't underestimate Joey, Barry. It won't bode well for you."

He laughs once again and sits back in his chair. "Money talks in Hollywood. The sooner she realizes that, the better we'll all be. Besides, you're the only couple still together from the original three and the fans are chomping at the bit to see what you're up to."

"They can watch TMZ or buy *People* magazine. The paparazzi are following us everywhere these days."

We stop talking when the waitress appears to refill our mugs. I tell her that I'd like a blueberry muffin when she gets a chance and Barry tells her he's fine.

"Of course they're following you. Everyone is waiting to see if you fuck it all up and leave your wife for Jules Maxwell." This time Barry isn't trying to hide the volume of his voice. A quick survey around the coffee shop tells me that no one is listening to us.

"And why would I do that?"

"For starters, you're having a child with Jules. People are placing bets on whether you bail and go back to her. Put her up in your fancy house in the Hills."

My stomach rolls and I want to hurl my coffee all over the table. Instead, I push it away, no longer interested. "Tell your friends that Jules isn't even on my radar. I'm more than happy with Joey."

"If that's what you think," he says, sighing. There's probably a reason this ass isn't married. Aside from being a chauvinistic pig, he's a complete douche.

"It's what I know. Are we done?"

"Nah, I have one more offer even though the first one still stands. We want the exclusive rights to your wedding. It'll be a six-week production schedule, we follow you both around while you get ready, film the wedding and the reception, and we'll air the ceremony on national television."

"For how much?"

"Ah, I see you're interested," he gloats. "We're offering a million, plus we cover all the expenses."

It's not enough, but I don't tell him that. "I'll talk to Joey and let you know."

"When's the wedding?"

I shake my head. "We haven't set a date, but it won't be in the US. We want a destination wedding, so that means you'll be covering the expenses of her family as well."

"Deal."

Except I never agreed. I only added terms. He slides a contract over to me and I leave it sitting on the table without even looking at it.

"Read and sign. My fax number is on the last page. Don't wait too long, though, Wilson. You have another woman waiting in the wings who is ready to make a huge production out of her pregnancy and you can bet she's already signed the contract."

Barry throws a few dollars down on the table and leaves. His last words replay over and over in my head. I should've known he'd go to Jules and she'd agree. Anything for her to be in front of the camera, making the masses feel sorry for her.

Before I can get up to leave, the waitress brings me my muffin. Instead of taking it to go, I let it sit in front of me, cooling down while I read over the contract. There are things that I have to do, but will need Joey's help and the first one is hiring a lawyer. A new agent needs to be sought out as well, especially before I sign any new deals. This is another reason why I don't want to start this movie—there are too many loose ends that have to be tied up. I can't do them if I'm working and Joey can't because she's not on all of my accounts. This is where Jason would come in, but I fired him months ago and haven't had the time to replace him.

I place a call to Blaze PR and ask them for a referral. Lucky for me, they have an in-house one and ask me to stop by and sign some papers so they can get my files from Jason. Unfortunately, I have to call him to let him know that he needs to comply as soon as possible or else. I'm not sure what the "else" is, but it sounded good when I said it. I make a few more calls, one of them being to Rob. We haven't spoken much since the night I moved out. I wasn't too thrilled to find Jules in the apartment. There wasn't a reason for her to be there. When she showed up, he should've told her to go home.

My call to Rob goes to voicemail. I don't leave him a

message—he'll know I called and if he wants to talk, he'll call me back.

"You look lonely."

I close my eyes at the sound of her voice and when I open them, she's sitting down. There's a large to-go coffee cup in her hand and a grin that matches the Cheshire cat.

"Far from it. I was just leaving."

"Well, being as you're alone, we should talk."

The Jules sitting across from me isn't the one I'm used to. Her hair isn't done up and her face lacks the mass of make-up she's usually wearing. Of course, the nails, jewelry, and designer handbag are all still there to help her accessorize.

"I know we need to talk, Jules, but I really don't have anything to say."

"We're having a baby, Josh. I'm fairly sure that means we have a lot to talk about."

"Right …" I fiddle with the rim of my coffee mug; the contents are cold and unwelcoming. My muffin mocks me. I'd wanted to eat it up until Jules sat down and now my appetite is long gone.

"This baby is a good thing for us, Josh."

I nod, unable to give her a verbal answer. It's not good, it's inconvenient and something I don't want with her. Hell, until I saw what a real family was like I didn't want kids, period. It's my wife who should be having them, not my ex. But that's not the baby's fault and he or she will never know my feelings on the situation.

"Anyway, you'll have to bond with the baby, so I figured that will start in the hospital and then we'll go home to my place. I think it's important that the baby know both of us, so you'll stay there."

My insides turn as she rambles on. I sit here, listening to her tell me about her fantasy world. Only in her mind does something like this work.

"I figure that you'll spend three to four nights at my

place. This way you're always there for our baby." She smiles as if this is the most amazing plan ever. By the time she's done talking, I've slouched in my chair and pulled my muffin apart.

"You know that won't work, Jules." I sit up and push my coffee out of my way. "I have a wife who expects me home every night and that is where I plan to be. I also expect my wife to be able to bond with the baby as well so when it's my days and nights to have the baby, he or she will come over to my house and bond with Joey and me."

Jules leans forward, squinting her eyes. "How many times have I told you that *she* is not allowed anywhere near my child?"

"Too many to count. How many times do you think I've given a shit about what you've said about her? None. You don't get to set rules and unreasonable expectations on me, Jules. If this is my child, I will have shared custody and Joey will be in their life."

"If?"

This the first time I've questioned whether or not the baby is mine. From the time she told me that she's pregnant I've believed it's my baby. I've let Joey plant doubt in my mind about me being the father.

"I want a paternity test, Jules."

Her mouth drops open and she lets out a gasp. "You think I would lie to you?"

"Yes. I think your actions during and after the show speak volumes about your character. I also can't recall the last time we slept together so that part is a little fuzzy."

"It's not safe for the baby, to do it during my pregnancy."

I nod, not knowing if she's telling the truth or not. "Well, I guess until then we have nothing to talk about." I go to stand, but she clamps her hand down onto my wrist.

"Josh, I would never lie to you. I know the things I did were underhanded but I was heartbroken. It should be me wearing your ring, not her. I don't believe you love her. Not like you love me."

Sitting back down, I face her. She doesn't let go of my hand and I don't want to make a scene so I let it stay. "That is where you're wrong, Jules. Joey … she's everything that I never knew I was missing. From the moment I kissed her on stage, I knew I was in trouble. We have a magnetic pull and it's constantly drawing me to her. I can't be away from her."

"You told Rob you were getting an annulment after the show." Her voice breaks and her eyes well with tears.

"That was the plan, but there was no way. I fell in love with her before I could even stop it."

"But you love me."

"I may have thought I did, and at one time it was probably true, but I haven't for a long time, Jules, and you know that. Things have never been the same since Bronx came into the picture. You chose to confide in him. You let him into our relationship. You did that. Not me. Joey isn't coming between us because there's nothing there. My heart, as much as I wanted to deny it, was open for her. I know this is hurting your feelings, but you need to realize that she's not going anywhere. She's not."

With that I get up and leave her at the table. Over the years I've consoled her, been her shoulder to cry on and her doormat. All of that ends here. It ends now.

Once I'm outside, I text Joey to let her know I'm on my way home after I stop at Blaze. I love typing that sentence: on my way home. Even in the short time that we've owned the house, she's made it ours. Her mom sent a slew of photos to us from the time we were there and Joey has framed and place them strategically around our house.

I know that she's not thrilled about the baby, but I have to commend her—the other day when I came home she was in one of our spare bedrooms taping paint to the wall for the baby's nursery. I realized in that moment I love her more and more each day. After I made love to her that night, I promised to give her a baby if that is what she wanted. I know she wants to be a mom, but now it's all up to her.

CHAPTER
nineteen

Joey

It's unrealistic to think that all of Josh's movies can be filmed on a back lot or on location in Los Angeles, and if I could have one wish that would be it because having him home every night has been a blessing. His filming schedule is hanging from the refrigerator. He put it there so we could plan dinner, or when we can meet up for lunch.

In the last month, everything has changed. We're domesticated and it feels odd, but it's a welcoming feeling that I'm falling in love with him more and more each day. We bought another car and he hired a cleaning service to come in once a week after I told him I clean a room a day to keep on top of the house. The house is enormous and too big for the two of us, even the three of us when the baby arrives.

Jules is still adamant that I have nothing to do with the baby and her court ordered paternity test went unanswered. I told Josh not to pressure her. It's her body and if she doesn't want to stick a mile-long needle into her abdomen then that should be her choice, even though I'm having a lot of reservations that she's even pregnant.

She shows up here randomly, takes shots at my character and expects me to wait on her. Her demands are never met, though, as Josh is always having to remind her of her place in our lives. But I've watched her when she's here and she's never rubbing her belly. Maybe it's just me and the copious amounts of Lifetime movies I've watched, but I never see her touching her stomach or asking Josh to feel the baby kick. He's even mentioned that at night when we're lying there and his hand is resting on my abdomen. His thumb will move back and forth along my skin, reassuring me that he wants us to have a child. I do, too, but not now. Part of me questions if he's only telling me this because of Jules. I want to ask him, but I don't want to hurt his feelings. Besides, he has enough on his plate. Josh doesn't need two screaming babies in the house with everything that is going on.

"What are you doing today?" Josh comes out of the closet, dressed in shorts and a tank top. My mouth waters at the sight of his biceps. There's a massive tattoo covering his shoulder and disappearing under his shirt. It's airbrushed for his movie, but that hasn't stopped me from pretending it's real. He's also growing, or maintaining facial hair. I've never been a huge fan of beards, but on him it's fucking sexy and I'm climbing him like a tree every night.

I close my eyes and count to ten, hoping to ward off the instant throbbing I feel for him.

"Going out with Rebekah."

Since coming back to L.A., we've spent time with Bronx and Rebekah. They come over for dinner, we go to their place, or we go out. While Rebekah and I have grown closer, Josh and Bronx are still pissing on each other for dominance, but they're at least cordial with each other.

Josh crawls onto the bed, hovering over me. He's already been reprimanded for being late and since then the studio decided to start sending a car for him. They figured if there were someone waiting, he wouldn't be late. They were wrong. My husband is insatiable.

"Where are you going?" He kisses my neck, tickling me with his beard.

"Shopping." I giggle, trying to get away from him, except he straddles me, pinning me between his legs.

"What are you buying me, something sexy, right?" He pulls the sheet down and cups my breasts before his fingers tweak my nipples.

"You're going to be late."

"I want you to be late."

"What?" I gasp as his tongue circles my nipple.

"I think you know what I mean." I do, but I'm more focused on the fact that the sheet I had covering my naked body is now pushed below my waist. The subtle hints aren't lost on me, but the timing isn't right. The drama that would ensue from us getting pregnant now would be too much to handle. The constant 'you treat your child better than you treat ours' would get tiring and the last thing I want is for Jules to use this baby against him. I know he's going to be a great dad. I also know he's been having conversations with my dad in regards to parenting. That alone is a huge step for Josh.

I look at the clock briefly, seeing that Josh is out of time. His driver will be here any second and he only waits a minute before he's ringing our doorbell. It's not only one ring and wait; it's the constant jab that makes the bell go off repeatedly.

"Don't start something you can't finish," I tell him, reaching into his shorts. The second my hand comes in contact with his shaft, his eyes roll back and his hips thrust, creating some friction.

He shimmies out of his shorts and boxers, letting his erection free and removing my hand. I adjust quickly, pulling my legs out from under him and spreading wide so his access to me is easy.

"Better make it quick, cowboy."

Smirking, Josh pats my clit with the head of his penis. "Maybe I want to tease you, make you suffer the way you make me suffer."

"I always give in."

"Not always," he says, slipping into me. "Sometimes you make me chase you, work for it." He pulls out, leaving me with a void. He's teasing, tormenting me. I'm worked up and he knows it. When he enters again, it's hard and eager, and suddenly my legs are up over his shoulders and he's pushing me forward.

"Fuck." I reach for any part of him: his ass, his arms, and even his side, anything that I can dig my fingers into for leverage.

"That's what I'm doing." He grunts and reaches for our headboard, using that to his advantage. The tightness builds quickly with the urgency of our situation. "Do you want to come?" he asks.

"Yes." I pant, my breathing labored as the familiar stirring starts to increase. His thumb presses down on my throbbing clit and I buck, desperately wanting more friction.

"Ah, Joey," he moans as my orgasm moves through my body. He moves faster, harder, and I take it, all of it.

"Josh," I whisper his name as he releases, grunting through the aftershocks that rock through our bodies.

"Fuck work," he says, falling off to the side. His shorts are barely below his ass, making him look like a horny teenager trying not to get caught by his girlfriend's dad.

"You say that every day."

"And I mean it every day."

The doorbell rings again; the loud annoying sounds grates on my nerves. "Fuck it," getting up off the bed, he pulls his shorts back up, "I'm going to work with your scent all over me."

I give him a look and he smirks. "I love the smell of your

pussy, so it's all good." He kisses me quickly and tells me that he loves me before rushing down the hall. I hear him faintly tell the driver good morning before the front door shuts.

"Do you like this one?"

I go over to where Rebekah is standing next to a white crib. It's pretty, but girlish. Our shopping adventure has landed us at a baby boutique. I've been eyeing this place for a while now, but haven't had the courage to go in. The baby is going to need things at our house, but deep down I don't want to buy the things I want my future child to have. I know it's selfish, but I want my son or daughter to have that special crib. I know I'm going to step mom hell.

"I really should wait for Josh. He should be picking this out, not me."

Sighing, Rebekah pulls me into her arms. The hug is friendly and needed. "Bronx doesn't think the baby is Josh's."

"I know, he's told me. Josh says she wouldn't lie about it, though, and the way she's been acting … I don't know. I question whether she's really pregnant."

"Hasn't Josh gone with her to an appointment or seen her sonogram?"

I shake my head. "He's asked, but there's always an ultimatum that goes with each request so he doesn't push her."

"Like what?"

We continue to browse through the store, my fingers touching over the soft fabrics used for blankets and clothes.

"She wants him to spend the night, all the time. Or go over to her place. When he says no, she withholds information about the baby and her pregnancy. She'll go on rants to him about how she's all alone, how I ruined her life and it will be a cold day in hell before she lets me hold her baby."

143

"But you let her into your house, Joey, why do you do that?"

Shrugging, I look away. Rebekah is a rarity in Hollywood according to Josh. She teaches Sunday school and has Bronx going to church twice a week. They don't party, unless they're at a friend's house, and she hardly ever drinks. I used to think her relationship with Bronx was all for the cameras and that her and Gary would end up together, but that's not the case. Sure, Gary wants her, but she's devoted to Bronx and their marriage.

"To keep the peace, I guess."

"Are you with her all the time when she's there?"

I shake my head. "No, she uses the bathroom. I don't follow her in there."

"I would," she mumbles before changing direction to look at the toys.

The thought sickens me that Jules would do something in my house that would hurt me, or even Josh. Maybe Rebekah is right and I've been too trusting of her. Maybe Josh has been as well.

As soon as Rebekah and I part ways I decide to head home, instead of going to the gym. When I step inside, my senses are heightened. I don't know what I'm looking for, but whatever it is needs to jump out and wave its hands for me.

Only one of the spare bedrooms has a bed and that room is right off the garage. I go in there and look over everything and see nothing out of place. I don't remember a time when she was gone longer than a few minutes, but I also don't remember tracking her time. I've been trying to give her the benefit of the doubt.

I go into the room that we'll be using for the baby's nursery. The paint samples I had taped to the wall are on the floor. I can't imagine she'd take them down. What purpose would that serve?

All the bathrooms are checked, but without knowing

what I'm looking for I can't be for certain she hasn't done anything.

The last room I check is our bedroom. My stomach drops at the thought of her being in here. The only thing I find out of place is the wedding photo on Josh's nightstand is turned backwards. I right it and wonder how long it's been like that.

Walking into my closet I roam over everything I have in there. It's mostly clothes with a few boxes of pictures that I haven't had a chance to go through yet. The garment bag that holds my wedding dress is there, visible for anyone who walks in. I know Josh wouldn't peek, but would she?

My heart drops as I start to pull the zipper down. I pray that Rebekah is wrong, but what if she isn't? What if I've been letting the devil play in my house? When the zipper reaches the bottom I push my hands inside the plastic and push it off the hangers.

I gasp and tears immediately take over my vision. My beautiful Cinderella dress is tattered and ripped to shreds. The beadwork on the bodice is pulled apart and the tulle is gone.

"Oh my God, she did this," I say out loud to my empty house. Bending down, I pick up the scraps of fabric and let them fall through my fingers. Beneath it all I find a stack of photos. Thumbing through them, the contents of my stomach stir. The pictures are of Jules on my bed, in my shower, and of her with Josh. There are numerous photos of Josh and Jules, sitting next to each other, taken inside this house when I'm not home or not in the room. He's smiling for the camera. Why?

I rush to the bathroom and expel my lunch. This woman is nothing but trouble in our lives and he continues to feed into her twisted reality. After rinsing my mouth, I trudge back to my closet for more torture, pausing at his. On his top shelf is a box that he keeps articles about himself in. I pull it down and open it.

My hand covers my mouth when I pick up the first one. It's about Josh and Jules going into a doctor's office. The picture attached shows them embracing. How did I miss all of this? Am I that blind that I can't even recognize when my husband is cheating on me?

I go back to the living room and grab my phone, dialing Bronx's number. He picks up on the second ring.

"Hey, what's up?"

"Is he cheating on me?"

"Josh? No, you know I'd tell you if he were. What's going on?"

"I found ... I ... oh God, he's been seeing her Bronx."

"Don't do anything, I'll be right over."

Bronx hangs up, but the damage is done. Everything is in black and white, printed for my viewing pleasure. My husband is a liar. Everything that I've been wishing for with him, he's been doing and lying to me about it all.

CHAPTER
twenty

Josh

When the driver pulls in, Bronx's car is in my driveway. I groan at the sight of it. I know Joey is friends with the Taylors, but I can only take so much of them. I don't care if she hangs out with Rebekah, but Bronx is another story.

I slam the door in frustration and the driver pulls away. I didn't even give him a chance to get out and open my door. After a long day of filming the last thing I want to do is deal with Bronx.

"Joey," I holler, slamming the door for effect. I want her to know I'm pissed. She should've texted me to give me a heads up that they're going to be here. I enter the living room, half expecting the windows to be open and to find them outside, but instead I'm met with Bronx sitting on my couch with a mess of something on the coffee table.

"Where's Joey?"

"Nice to see you, too." He doesn't move from my couch. In fact, he crosses his leg over his other as if he's welcome to stay.

"Where's Joey?" I ask again.

He shakes his head and sighs, pissing me off even more. My day was utter shit and I just want to crawl into bed with my wife and forget everything.

"She left."

"What do you mean she left?"

"I mean Joey decided to look at her wedding dress today and found it ripped to shreds, along with an assortment of fucking photos of you and Jules. And because that wasn't enough torture, she decided to go snooping in your closet and found an article about you and Jules going to a doctor's appointment so she fucking left you, Josh," he says, standing.

"I warned her about you and Jules, but she wouldn't listen. And when Jules said she was pregnant I told you both that it's not yours, but you have the gall to tell Joey that Jules wouldn't lie to you? Look at this mess, Josh. Do you think Joey tore up her own fucking dress? Do you think she took pictures of Jules lying on your bed? When did you think it would be okay for you and Jules to pose for pictures while you're cuddled up on your couch? Newsflash, buddy, it's never fucking okay. You should've let Joey go when the show ended."

I'm trying to digest Bronx's words, but they're muted and mumbled. I can't get past keywords of Joey being gone, her dress being ruined, and Jules. I can see the picture on the table, but my vision is blurred from a mixture of tears and anger. Why would Joey leave and not talk to me about this first?

Because she's been down this path before, that's why. And I promised to never do that to her.

"Where is she, Bronx?"

He shrugs. "I'm not fucking telling you."

"She's my wife," I say with authority. "I have a right to know."

"Your rights sailed when you stuck your dick back into Jules. Here's what I don't get, Josh. Joey fucking loves you. She worships the ground you walk on, why do this to her? Why fill her head with false promises?"

"I didn't. I do love her. This shit with Jules …" I pick up a photo—it's of her and me together, but I don't remember taking it. "I didn't take these and I haven't been to any appointments with her."

"There's proof," he says, picking up the heap on the table and dropping it back down. "How do you explain all of this? And her dress, Josh? Joey opened her fucking home to that witch and this is how she repays her?"

I sit down and rake my hands over my face, groaning out loud in frustration. "The dress was in Joey's closet, which would mean Jules went in there on one of the nights she showed up here." I pick up a tattered piece of her dress; it's an off-white, almost beige color and reminds me of the champagne we shared after she agreed to marry me again. Tears prickle my eyes as I clutch the fabric to my chest.

"I didn't cheat, nor did I lie to her," I tell Bronx even though I don't owe him anything. "I'm so in love with her, it hurts. I physically ache when she's not near me, and knowing that I knocked up Jules kills me inside every single day. I know its destroying Joey, too. I would never do this to her, go to those appointments and not tell her."

"Yeah, well, it sure looks like it."

The photos are spread out all over the couch, mocking me. I pick up a few and feel the bile burning my throat. Jules spread out on our bed in nothing but a shirt with her bulging belly sticking up. She's smiling, like this is some kind of game to her. But who took the photo? When was she in our house when we weren't home?

"The baby isn't yours, Josh."

"Why do you keep saying that? Is it to give Joey hope that this nightmare goes away?"

149

He shakes his head and sits back down on the couch as if he's welcome. He's not. I want him to leave after he tells me where to find my wife.

"Because I was with her the night before I met Rebekah, which happens to be about a month before you went on the show. I made the mistake of bringing Jules back to my apartment. We had been drinking and shit started getting heavy. She's a sure fucking thing, so I fucked her."

"You son of a bitch! This whole time I'm sweating bullets, trying to reassure my wife that I'm devoted to her and you're the fucking father?"

"No, I'm not. When I was with her she had an implant in her arm. I'm not a fucking doctor, but unless she took it out and you have miracle sperm I doubt she can be pregnant by you."

It's the same shit he's been spewing to Joey for months, but I haven't listened because I wanted to trust Jules. We had been together, but I can't recall when the last time was. I know we had been and I hadn't been using a condom. That thought alone makes my stomach roll.

"I don't have a clue who she was with while I was in the house."

"It wasn't me. I know you have a hard time believing that Rebekah and I are married, but it's true. The Rebekah I met isn't the one you and Joey know. She had purple hair and wanted to party. The best part about her, she didn't have a fucking clue who I was and that made everything more enticing with her. The one-night stand turned into a weekend and three weeks later she's telling me that she's pregnant. She hadn't left my side so I knew it was mine. We went down to the justice of the peace and got married."

"Rebekah's pregnant?"

He shakes his head. "About two weeks before Barry called us, she miscarried and said it was a sign that her wild ways were over. Dyed her hair back to her natural color and started making me go to church."

"Holy shit, but I'm confused. I thought you told Joey that you met Rebekah at church?"

"I did because I wasn't about to out our secret on national television. No one knows about the miscarriage and I want to keep it that way. Rebekah knows I'm a sinner. Hell, she was, too, but has been repenting ever since. She thinks it's her fault she lost the baby even when I tell her that these things happen and we can try again. When it comes down to it, she loves me and I love her, even if we started off backwards. It killed me when she lost the baby, though, and that's when I woke up. I realized that what we were building was worth something and I didn't want to lose it."

I process everything he's telling me, and as much as I don't want it to, it does change the way I see him and Rebekah. The last thing I want to be is a friend to Bronx, but I think I'm outvoted by my conscience on this one.

"You know Jules and I had broken up before I met Barry in the bar. I told her I was done with her, but she still came around. I was so stupid to think she was pining away for me. Every time we'd hook-up, she'd insinuate that we were together and I'd blow her off. Jules never took no for an answer."

"This could easily be a way to get revenge on you."

"I blew her off for Joey on the day of the finale," I tell him. He knows how I feel about that day, the one that he ruined. That should've been our first night together without cameras following our every move. Instead, I was holed up in a hotel room trying to do everything I could to find her.

I look at the mess on the table and wonder how I could be so fucking stupid to believe her. And I let her into our home, under the assumption that we were going to be parents, and this is how she repays me? By destroying Joey's wedding dress?

"I'm so fucked."

"Pretty much. Joey is devastated. I don't think she cared too much about the dress, but the pictures and knowing that Jules was in her house when she wasn't home—that killed her."

"Unless she broke in, she's never been here unless Joey and I were home. I wouldn't let her in if Joey weren't here. I don't know where these pictures are coming from." I glance at them and decide to turn them over. I don't want to see them. I don't want the reminder that my wife walked out on me because of them.

"Do you know where she is?" I ask again, hoping that he'll tell me this time.

He shakes his head. "I don't. I arrived, consoled her, and she left. I decided to stay so you wouldn't worry about her."

"Yet I am."

"I know, but at least you know why she's not here." He points to the mess on the table. "I gotta run, Rebekah's waiting for me at home." Bronx stands and takes a few steps toward the door.

"I still don't like you, but thank you."

"As long as you tolerate me for your wife, I don't care. Joey means a lot to me and I don't want to see her hurting."

"She means everything to me," I mutter as the front door closes. I lean back and scream until my throat feels raw. Tears fall down the side of my face as I stare at the ceiling. What a fucking mess my life is when it should all be so easy. Joey and I should be figuring out what to eat, instead my house is empty and my wife isn't home.

Making my way to the bedroom, I head for her closet. Most of her hangers are empty.

"She left me."

My hand flies through the empty hangers as I swing my arm out at the mass. Some fall to the floor, but others bounce back and snap into my skin leaving a welt. "Fuck," I scream, pounding my fist into the wall.

I reach for my phone and bring it to life. Both my screensaver and background picture are of her and I keep one screen clear of any icons so I can stare at this picture in particular. I took it the morning after we bought the house. She was just waking up and looked so beautiful. I had to capture the moment.

Pressing the phone icon, I tap on her name. Her phone rings, but goes to voicemail. I know I should leave her a message, but I'm not sure what to say right now. Sorry doesn't cut it.

Traipsing back into the living room, I gather the pictures and article and set them aside. I'm going to have to ask Jules about all of this, but right now I want to get the mess cleaned up in case she comes home.

When I scoop up what's remaining of her dress the label catches my eye. I know I can at least fix this for her. I sit down and quickly Google the name on the label. As soon as they answer I tell them who I am and how I need a custom dress for my wife to wear when we renew our vows. The designer's assistant is all too eager to make sure Joey has the dress of her dreams. Before we hang up I tell her what she's looking for and when we need it by. I know Joey doesn't want to do the reality shit with our lives, but I think letting Barry do our wedding is something we need. I want her to be treated like a princess and I can't do that alone.

My next call is to Barry, letting him know that I'm on board and that Joey will be. I need a week to convince her. When he asks when the wedding is, I tell him seven weeks. He mutters some curse words, but wants the exclusive so I know he's game. I tell him Hawaii is where we want to get married at sunset. More words follow about lighting and staging, which I ignore. I know he'll get it done.

As soon as I hang up with him, I call Jules. The sound of her voice is like nails on the chalkboard.

"It's official," I tell her.

"What is?"

"You're the biggest bitch I have ever met and I regret ever being introduced to you."

"Joshieee," she whines, dragging my name out.

"No, Jules, you need to listen because I'm only saying this once. This shit you're pulling stops now. I'm calling my lawyer and having you held for contempt or whatever the fuck it's called. I want a paternity test done now. I'm also calling the police and having my house dusted for your fingerprints, especially on Joey's dress. This shit is so fucking childish. You're an adult, it's time you grow up and act like one."

"Josh, I didn't—"

"Don't tell me you didn't do anything. You just admitted it. If you weren't guilty you would've asked what happened, but you already know. I'm done, Jules. If the baby is mine, we'll share custody, but until I know for certain I don't want you anywhere near me."

I hang up before she has a chance to say anything. It's not going to matter what she says, I don't believe her. Not anymore.

My final call is to Joey and this time I leave a message, telling her how sorry I am that I ever met Jules and that I promise to make it up to her. I assure her that I'm not cheating, nor have I cheated since the day I kissed her on stage under the lights with the audience watching. By the time I've hung up and called back three times, I'm running out of things to say aside from I'm sorry, I'll fix everything and that I love her. My last words to her are, "We're doing the production of our wedding if you don't call me back." If that doesn't do the trick I don't know what will.

CHAPTER
twenty-one

Joey

For three days I avoid him. The phone calls, the text messages, they all went unanswered. I even went as far to deactivate the GPS on my phone so he couldn't find me. I thought about running, but made it as far as the ocean before I stopped. The beach was calling me and I thought I'd find peace here. For the three days that I ignored Josh, I sat on the beach with my toes in the sand, watching the waves crash into the sand and listening to the seagulls and families around me live life.

When the sun would set and the bonfires would start I stayed in the shadows, remembering a time in my life when this was the norm. The young couples flirting and falling in love—that was me once, and when it went to shit I thought I'd never find it again. I want the laughter, the dancing around, and the kisses by the fire. I want my friends gathered around telling stories of our younger days while our partner holds us. It may seem too simple for some, but for me it's how I always pictured things would be. I want simple and not hectic, and I suppose being married to Josh Wilson it has to be the latter because his life is crazy.

When I met Josh I knew he was too good to be true, but I still hoped. I still thought I deserved some sort of happiness. I've listened to his messages, read them, too. Some were frantic while others calm. The threat of another television show is there and that means I have to make a decision. Do I stay married to Josh or do I end it? I honestly have no idea what will be better for me. I'm deeply in love with him and I know he loves me, but I'm not sure if it's enough.

I don't want to be in a relationship where I'm second-guessing everything. Josh says he didn't cheat and I want to believe him. Deep in my heart I know he's telling the truth, but my brain can't accept it. My mind keeps playing scenarios over and over in my head. What if I go home now and Jules is there? What if she's in my house, my room and taking over my life because I can't seem to find the resolve to get up and listen to my husband?

Wiping my tears with the backs of my hands, careful not to get sand in my face, I finally stand and head back to my car. It was easy to find a hotel along the beachfront, but I hated being there without Josh. I wanted to experience the serene beauty of the ocean with him; walk on the sandy beaches and play in the waves. At night I longed for his touch and often lay there listening to the ocean when I should've been sleeping.

The drive back to our house is done without the chatter of the radio. I need to think about the words that I want to say, to tell him how I feel and be confident in the decision that I'm making when I step in the door, because even as I pull into my driveway I don't know what I'm going to say or do. I don't know if I'm going to stay here any longer.

No sooner do I shut my car door do I find Josh standing in the doorway, watching me. His eyes are bloodshot; he looks pale and I think he's lost some weight. He doesn't move when I reach the entryway, instead he stares at me, his eyes move over my body as if he's inspecting me.

Words are caught in my throat when he pulls me to his chest in a crushing hug. My response is automatic as my arms wrap around him, gripping his shirt in my fists. When he lets out a sob, I follow quickly. I don't know how long we stand there crying in each other's arms, but it's a while and it's worth it.

He takes me by the hand, leading me into our house. The last time I was here, I was breaking down in front of Bronx while I showed him everything, each piece of evidence worse than the others, but nothing could even come close to what Jules had done to my wedding dress.

When we get to the living room, the existing black sectional we had has been replaced with a white one with red accent pillows.

"If you don't like it, we can go pick something out together."

I nod, unable to form any words right now. He continues to take me to our bedroom. I stop suddenly and gasp. Our navy blue comforter has been changed to a dark purple, the same colors in our bathroom. Tears well in my eyes and when I look at Josh, he's crying, too.

"I don't know how she got in, but I changed the locks as well. I also called the police and filed a report against her. Baby, you have to believe me, I didn't cheat. Hell, I didn't even pose for those pictures. I don't know where she got them from or how she got into our house, but it'll never happen again."

I wander around the room, wondering what else she has tainted. I have never met someone so evil before. Sure I've read stories about women like her, but to encounter one? There are no words to describe the agony she's put me in.

Sitting down on the side of the bed, Josh sits down beside me.

"You changed the bedding?"

"All of it. I threw everything away, too. I didn't want any memories of her around this house."

"But there will be when the baby comes."

"Not if it's not mine. Bronx and I had a long talk. I can see why you're friends with him. And while I may never be, he opened my eyes to a lot of the stuff Jules has done in the past. I was stupid to trust her. She has to take the paternity test tomorrow."

"What happens if she doesn't?"

He shakes his head. "I guess they put her in jail. I don't know."

I let out a strangled laugh, covering my mouth. "Jules in jail would be a funny sight."

"Yeah, well, we won't be visiting her."

I shake my head, agreeing with him. Letting out a yawn, I move to lie down. I'm so tired, both mentally and physically. Josh sneaks in, spooning me from behind.

"I'm so sorry, Joey. I feel like I've done nothing but apologize since we got together. I hope you know how hurt I am that she did this to us ... to you. I told her I'm done, that her and I are no longer on speaking terms and I questioned whether I'm the father or not. Bronx really thinks I'm not."

"I know. I told you that but you wouldn't listen."

Josh sighs and digs his face into my neck. "I'm an idiot. I honestly can't blame you if you leave me."

"Is that what you want?"

He rolls me over so we can face each other. "Hell no. Joey, since I came home and found Bronx here I've been a fucking mess. Every day ... hell, probably ten times a day, I texted him asking if he's heard from you so I know if you're okay. I hated that you left your home because of the cancer I brought into our lives. God, baby, you're everything to me and if I have to spend the rest of my life making up for Jules and her bullshit, I will."

Josh pushes my hair behind my ear and my eyes close at the simple gesture. When I look at him his eyes have changed from sadness to longing. "Being without you these past few days have been torture. I show up on set looking like a fucking mess and my day doesn't get much better. Coming home to an empty house is the worst possible feeling when I know I could've prevented this. Everything that happened is my fault and I'm sorry."

"Did you go to the doctors with her?"

He shakes his head. "Never. The only place outside of our home that I have seen Jules without you is the day before filming at the coffee shop. She showed up after I had a meeting with Barry. I told her then, the same thing I've told her repeatedly, that I'm in love with you and she needed to learn to accept that because it wasn't going to change."

I lean into Josh and let him hold me. The warmth of this touch, the calmness of his breathing and the way his body intermingles with mine lulls me to sleep. It's restless, but still more than I've had in the past few days.

When I wake, I'm alone. The wall of windows is open and I can see the soft glow of the fireplace outside. Josh is sitting by the fire, spread out on the couch with his feet hanging over the edge.

"Hey," I say, trying to alert him to my presence.

"Hey." He sits up and pats the spot next to him. "How'd you sleep?"

"Better than I have the past few days."

"Yeah I haven't slept at all."

I don't know what I'm supposed to say to that so I stay tight-lipped and focus on the flame coming out of the fireplace.

"I'm sorry for leaving, Josh. There really isn't an excuse other than I panicked and was really fed up with all the shit going on surrounding her."

"I know. I don't blame you, Joey. I only wish you had

called."

Shaking my head, I pull my legs up and wrap my arms around them. "I couldn't. I'd hear your voice and forget why I left and I'd be back to square one."

"I figured."

"Thing is, I never asked to be matched to you, that was done for us and I couldn't be happier. I love you. I've fallen so deeply in love that nothing should matter, except it does. I can't have her in my life, ruining everything. She's the type of person that if you give her an inch, she's taking a mile. First it's my dress, next it will be a vacation, or down the road Christmas morning."

Josh pulls me into his lap and holds me. "I promise I won't let that happen. If, and it's a big if, the baby is mine we'll have a custody agreement in place. My new lawyer says those are pretty solid so if she violates it, she can go to jail."

"What do you mean, 'big if'?"

He sighs and kisses my cheek. My whole body reacts, screaming at me to kiss him back, but I hold back. "Bronx shared some information and the likelihood that the baby is mine is very slim. I already went down to the hospital and did the DNA swab and I paid to have a rush job done so we should know once she does her part tomorrow."

"Do you know how foolish I'll feel if the baby isn't yours?"

"You?" he asks, laughing. "I've been walking on eggshells for months because I didn't want you to leave me. You're not leaving me, are you?" His words are hopeful, yet pleading.

"No, I'm not."

"That's good, because we start filming on Monday for our show."

"Josh," I whine. He knows how I feel about filming another reality show.

"Babe, listen. Barry is paying for everything. We're going to Hawaii, all of us; your whole family, and I even included Bronx and Rebekah. You don't have to do anything except tell people what you want. And your mom will be here at the end of next week to help you."

"Really?"

He nods and plasters the sweetest grin on his face. "Yep, and I called the designer of your dress, you have a meeting with them next week to get fitted for something new."

"Josh," I gasp, covering my mouth as I try to ward off the tears. "Seriously?"

"Joey, I only want to make you happy. I know being in front of the camera again isn't something you want to do, but you're getting your dream wedding and you won't have to lift a finger. You get to bark orders at others and snap your fingers when you want something done."

"That's not really me though."

"I know, but for a few weeks it can be and you can do it with a smile."

Taking his hand in mine, I attempt to tug him off the couch. "Come on." I motion with my head toward our room.

"Nah, get back here," he says, pulling me back onto his lap. "I haven't been with you for three days, Joey, and that is far too long. Tonight, I'm going to make love to you under the stars."

"Outside?" I ask, unsure how I feel about this.

"Right here on this couch."

"What if someone sees us?"

Josh looks around and smirks. We have trees that block the backyard from prying eyes and an electric fence that runs along our privacy fence. Logistically the only way they'd see us if they climb on to their roof and still then our roof gets in the way.

"You know it's safe."

I nod, biting my lower lip. "I do."

Closing his eyes, he leans his forehead against mine. "I can't wait to hear you say that again. Only seven weeks from now and those sweet words will come from your lips once again, but this time you'll be looking into my eyes when you say it."

"And your soul."

Josh kisses me, slowly, testing the waters so to speak. But it's not enough for me. He may think he's the only one addicted in our relationship, but he's sorely mistaken.

CHAPTER
twenty-two

Josh

Knocking on my former apartment door seems odd, but the last thing I want to do is barge in if Rob's busy. I'm going to ask him to be my best man, but his answer will depend on his response to my questions about Jules. I still clearly remember the day Joey and I walked in and Jules was sitting too close for comfort to my best friend. They've been friends for a long time, but since that day something hasn't sat very well with me.

"Why are you knocking?" Rob asks, standing there in nothing but a pair of shorts. His hair is wet and there's a towel resting on his shoulders. I glance over the wrought iron railing and look down at the pool. It's full of girls, who all wave up when they see me.

"Not my place anymore. I don't want to interrupt anything." Stepping in, I close the door behind me. I wish I could say the place has changed, but nothing has. I think if Rob had moved out I'd rearrange or buy something new.

"You're always welcome."

"Unless you're getting laid. I don't want to walk in on that shit."

Rob laughs and offers me something to drink. "Something mellow. I'm driving." He returns and hands me a bottle of water, while he kicks back with a beer. I do miss hanging out with him and need to make sure our friendship doesn't suffer because I'm married and changing my path. He's still my best friend and I don't want to lose sight of that.

"How's married life? Is it worth it?"

"Is it worth what?"

"Giving up the unlimited amount of free pussy?"

I try to laugh it off, but that's who Rob is. He uses his status as an aspiring and upcoming actor to get laid. He scores more when he's with me, though, because he's not afraid to mention who his best friend is.

"Definitely, as long as it's Joey."

"And Jules?"

Fiddling with the label on my water, I meet his gaze. "That's why I'm here. What's going on with you guys?"

He looks at me and shakes his head. "Nothing, man. I wouldn't do that to you."

"She's not mine."

"And I'm not hers."

"The day Joey and I bought the house, she was here. It looked like she was sitting close to you. It makes me wonder. She's a beautiful woman, so I wouldn't blame you."

"Except she's hung up on you and pregnant. Besides, that day you showed up, she had been waiting here for hours. Every single day she was coming over to see if you were here. Jules was crying and thought my shoulder was the place to seek solace. I didn't touch her. Never have and never will." Rob heads back to the kitchen and returns with another beer. "How's Joey taking that anyway?"

Twisting the cap on my bottle, I down about half the contents before setting it down on my knee. "Jules is hung on anyone who wants to give her attention. As far as Joey and the Jules situation it's complicated, but Joey's a strong woman and knows that I love her."

"I think the best decision you ever made was staying with Joey. She seems nice. I'd like to get to know her." Any doubt I had about Rob being interested in Jules, or hooking up with her is long forgotten. He's my best friend and they don't do that shit to friends. He knows I'd never do that to him.

"Well that's why I'm here. In six weeks we're getting married, or renewing our vows, and I'd like to know if you'd be my best man?"

"Hell yeah," he says, standing. I do the same and we hug. "Are you pissed she wants a wedding?"

"It's not her, it's me, man. I'm so in love with her that I want to watch her walk down the aisle. I want to see her face when she says her vows to me. The first time was a joke." I shrug. "I mean, we're married, but her ring was tiny and there was no emotion in our vows. I want the real thing."

"Dude, you're pussy whipped."

We both sit back down and I start laughing. "You know it, and I'll fucking admit it. She's the best damn thing that has ever happened to me."

"What do your parents think of her?"

I glance at him and shake my head. "I don't even know if they know I'm married. Neither of them has called for money lately, and I really have no reason to call them. I should, though. Maybe we'll video chat with them later."

"Better warn them first because I'm sure they'll have a few negative things to say."

He's right, and that is the main reason I haven't told them. Their lives are screwed up. I have no doubt my mom will see her money tree slipping away, and that will be Joey's fault, and knowing my father he'd probably try to hit on her with me sitting right next to her. Hell, they don't even know about the possibility of me becoming a father. Not that it would matter—they'll never have anything to do with any of my children.

"You should come over for dinner," I offer to Rob. "Come see the house, go for a swim."

Laughing, he pulls at his shorts. "Yeah, I think I'll do that."

I finish the rest of my water and take my empty bottle into the kitchen. "I gotta run. I have to pick up Joey and we're meeting with my lawyer about Jules."

"What'd she do?"

"Court ordered paternity test. I wasn't going to push the issue because she said it wasn't safe for the baby, but she somehow broke in and planted a bunch of pictures and shit, and destroyed Joey's wedding dress. I'm done with her, man."

"See what I'm talking about," he replies, standing. "Love makes you crazy."

I don't want to call what Jules has done love. You don't hurt the people you love. I get that she feels scorned and that's my fault for giving her false hope. When we broke up I should've stopped sleeping with her, answering her calls, and hanging out with her. I led her on and that has proven to come back and bite me in the ass.

"Are you nervous?" Joey asks, leaning her head on my shoulder. We're in the office of our new lawyer, waiting to find out if Jules' baby is mine. If it's mine, I'll deal, but I'm praying that it isn't. Not because I don't want to be a dad, but because I want Joey to be the one who gives me my first child and I really want Jules to be out of our lives once and for all. I know I created the way she is by my actions and if I could change it I would, but I can't. I made stupid choices and I'm hoping they stop coming back to bite me in the ass.

"Yes and no."

"Why the no?"

"Because of what Bronx told me. He's pretty sure that I'm not the father and even questioned if she's truly pregnant."

"I've said the same thing." Her fingers dance along my arm, roaming up and down. Her touch is soothing and something I crave daily. Joey is like my own personal source of oxygen. I don't know how I ever considered myself to be living before I met her.

"I know, but she's big."

"And never touches her belly. When skin stretches it hurts, and when she was at our house she never asked you to feel the baby moving. I found that odd."

"And that is something I didn't even notice."

We're not the only ones waiting in the office. I'm trying to avoid looking around the room, not wanting to make eye contact with anyone, but it's too late. As soon as I glance to my right there's a woman staring and checking her phone. When she starts to stand, I sit up, causing Joey to move her head.

"Are you Josh Wilson?"

When they ask like that I've been tempted to say no, to see what they'd say, but I don't want to be rude.

"I am."

"Oh my God. I can't believe this. Here I am waiting to file for divorce and you're sitting right here. You're my favorite actor."

Joey snickers beside me and I give her a knowing look.

"Thank you."

"And you're Joey?"

Now it's me laughing. She's always joked that no one will ever recognize her so she doesn't need a disguise when she goes out. Not that I have one on aside from a baseball hat.

"I am," she replies, beaming. I'm smiling too because I believe this is her first fan encounter and it's a positive one.

"Can I get a photo with the both of you?"

"Absolutely," I say, speaking for Joey as well. "Excuse me, can you take our photo?" I ask the man sitting across from us. He seems bothered by my question, but stands anyway. The fan hands him her phone.

I stand and her arm comes around me instantly. I try to put a little separation between us, but she moves closer, clearly needing to be inside my bubble.

"What side do you want me on?" Joey asks. The fan holds her other arm out, showing Joey where she wants her.

We stand for a few seconds smiling until the man hands her the phone back.

"Wow, thank you so much." She starts to walk away and as we're sitting back down she turns. "Wait, you guys aren't getting a divorce, are you?"

"No, just signing some paperwork."

"Oh phew. You guys were my favorite couple on *Married Blind.*"

"Thanks. And hey, if you're interested, we start filming a new show next week. It'll be live for the most part as we get ready to renew our vows."

"I'll be front row and center," she exclaims, sitting back down. Her attention is solely on her phone now.

"She's happy," Joey says, leaning into me again.

"Even though she's here to get a divorce, we made her day."

Within seconds both our phones go off with notifications. We laugh as we check and find that she's posted our picture on Instagram.

"I'm commenting," Joey says, much to my surprise. I'm smiling when her comment on how excited she was to meet the woman today shows up, and a quick glance across the room tells me that Joey has made her day even brighter.

"That was nice of you." I kiss her on her forehead instead of the lips. As much as I want to do the latter I don't want that picture out there.

168

Joey shrugs. "She wanted me in her photo, it's the least I could do."

"Mr. and Mrs. Wilson, if you'll follow me."

Joey and I wave at our fan and head through the door, following our attorney's secretary. She shows us into his office where we take a seat, joining hands immediately. Regardless of the outcome, we're in this together. And if the baby is mine, we're filing for custody and asking the judge to take into consideration Jules' mental state and her actions inside our home.

"I bet you're anxious." Dan Woodstock came highly recommended by Blaze, making my decision to sign with him easy. Since then, Joey and I have changed all of my necessary paperwork and added her name. Before, my estate—for it's worth—was going to my parents and the community center. Now everything will go to Joey. The community center will still benefit, but it will be at her discretion in the event she's supporting our children. I'm planning ahead, even if she isn't yet.

Dan opens the large manila envelope, causing my heart to start racing. I've never been more nervous than I am now. Even when I married Joey my body didn't shake with anticipation like this.

"I feel like I should be on the Maury Povich show," I blurt out, squeezing Joey's hand. Both she and Dan laugh, but I don't find it funny. My life hangs in the balance of what that piece of paper says.

"The alleged father, Joshua Wilson, can be excluded as the biological father of the fetus here by referred to as Baby Maxwell."

"Holy shit, she is pregnant," Joey says.

"I'm sorry, what?" I ask, swallowing hard. I don't think I heard him correctly.

"You're not the father, Josh," Joey says with tears in her eyes.

"I'm not?"

She shakes her head, biting her lower lip. "You're not."

I sit back in the chair, letting the words sink in.

"Holy shit."

"Yeah, your wife already said that. I think this is cause for celebration?" Dan asks.

"Fuck yeah it is."

We both stand and I shake his hand, probably too aggressively, but I don't care. I'm fucking happy. And before I leave the room, I pick Joey up and spin her around.

"The baby … it's not mine."

"I know." I gently let her down, and she cups my face with her hands, smiling. "No lies here, Josh, but I'm really happy."

"Me too, babe. Now we can make our own."

There's a sparkle in her eye telling me that yes, we're going to start trying. Not that we haven't been trying this whole time, but she's still on the pill. Maybe when we get home we can have a ceremony for getting rid of those tiny pills that keep blocking my sperm from knocking her up.

CHAPTER
twenty-three

Joey

I'm giddy, yet saddened by the desperate attempts Jules has made in her efforts to keep Josh away from me. To use an innocent baby is deplorable in my mind, yet I know it happens all the time.

Inside our home, I breathe a sigh of relief. The nightmare is over, although I don't expect Jules to go away anytime soon. They're still in the same social circle and will be at the same industry events. It's too much to wish that we'd never run into her. Except when we do, I hope that she saves face and avoids us. Lying for months about who the father of your baby is … I can't even.

"Who do you think the father is?" I ask Josh, who is busy trying to pick up our house. The cleaning lady doesn't come until tomorrow and he's invited Rob over, which subsequently lead to us inviting Rebekah and Bronx over as well. After a stop at the grocery store to pick up food and beverages, we're home and scrambling to be ready for our company.

"Matt," he replies, shocking me. My mouth drops open

and he uses his finger to push it closed.

"What, why?"

"I don't know." He shrugs and proceeds to load the dishwasher with our mugs from this morning. "The whole mess in Alabama has never sat well with me. Why betray me for her, ya know?"

"I don't know, babe. I mean, there seems to be a lot of that going on in the industry, right?"

"Unfortunately." He sounds sad and that breaks my heart. I know he was close to Matt and Jason, but they've done things to him that haven't been in his best interests. Josh comes to me as I lean up against the counter, watching him.

"You're the best thing that has ever happened to me," he says, wrapping his arms around my waist.

"That's not true. If you hadn't become an actor, I doubt our paths would've ever crossed." My hands rub up and down on his chest until I lock them behind his neck.

"Is that what you think?"

I nod. "We'd have to have a lot of stars align for us."

"Not necessarily. Can you imagine if I signed up for the show and we were matched. Would you still have fallen for me if the circumstances were changed? If I weren't the Joshua Wilson that hangs in poster form on your wall?"

"Would you have the same personality?"

He laughs. "And the same looks."

I run my fingers through his hair and lean forward to kiss him. "Then yeah, I'd fall for you. Aside from your job, once I got to know the person you are in the inside, it changed everything for me."

He lifts me up onto the counter so we're eye level. Smooth fingers push my hair behind my ear and beautiful brown eyes gaze deep into mine. "You make me want to be sappy and profess feelings that I never thought I'd feel. And that all started when I kissed you the first time. Even though

172

I thought I could be strong around you, all you have to do is say my name and I'm putty in your hands."

"Good knowledge for the future."

"Speaking of," he says, sighing. "I know it's not only my choice, but I'd really like for you to go off the pill. We really haven't discussed it and I don't want you to think this is in reaction to the whole Jules saga. When I saw you with your family I knew that it's something I wanted to give you."

"When you say it's not a reaction to Jules, do you mean because she was pregnant or because the baby isn't yours? I don't want to get pregnant and have a baby only for you to realize months down the road that you truly don't want to be a father."

Josh cups my cheek and holds his hand there for a moment before kissing me lightly. "When I found out Jules was pregnant, the first thing I thought was it should've been you even if I didn't want it. You should've been the one to have my baby. That inkling turned to desire, and before I knew it I was picturing you with a small bump and saw us shopping for the perfect crib for our baby."

A smile spreads across my face, causing Josh to step back in what I'm assuming is in confusion.

"I went off the pill about a month ago."

"You did?"

I nod, biting my lower lip.

"How long does it take?"

"I don't know, but practicing will help I'm sure." I wink teasingly. He scoops me up and I squeal, wrapping my legs around him. We're only halfway down the hall when the doorbell rings. We both groan, but know that we invited people over so we don't have a choice but to answer the door. That's one of the beauties about where we live—you can't show up unless you're on our list. Security is twenty-four seven and everyone must check in.

"I love you, Mrs. Wilson," he says, kissing me chastely

before putting me down.

"I love you, Mr. Wilson." We're silly and ridiculous with how we act and we don't care. We didn't get that year long—or longer is some cases—courtship, and almost everything we do is new.

Josh opens the door to let Bronx, Rebekah, and Rob in. It's funny how they arrived at the same time, but whatever works. Bronx and Rebekah give me a hug, and Bronx hangs on a bit longer until Josh is clearing his throat.

"Come on, let's get outside," Josh says, showing Rob the way to go.

"Wow, your house is amazing."

"Thanks, man. It feels good to be a homeowner."

As soon as we step out onto the patio, Josh is getting us all beer. He pops the tops and calls us all in.

"Joey and I want to thank you for being here tonight. Not only are we celebrating our last days away from the camera, but we also found out today that I'm not the father of Jules's baby. Bronx, I want to thank you for everything."

We all click our bottles together and take a drink.

"You dodged a bullet there, man," Rob says, patting him on the back.

"Don't I know it," Josh sighs. "Let me show you around." He motions for Rob to walk back into the house while Bronx, Rebekah, and I take a seat around the fireplace.

"Are you happy, Joey?" Bronx asks.

"Yes, I am. I mean, I would've accepted my fate if the baby turned out to be his, but now it finally feels like our lives are starting. We have nothing looming in front of us, aside from this production, and I feel like I can breathe again. No more eggshells or wondering what she's going to do and say next."

Bronx smiles and leans into Rebekah. For the longest time I couldn't figure these two out, but they seem to work and I like her, despite her attempt to kill me in the house.

"Have you heard from Millie?" Rebekah asks.

I shake my head and instantly feel like shit that I haven't checked in with her. "I talked to her a day or so before we found out about Jules and I've been so busy that I haven't had time to catch up with her. Gah, I'm a shitty friend."

"Or you were worrying about your life first. Nothing wrong with that, Joey," Bronx says, defending my actions.

"What about Gary? Have you talked to him?" If anyone thought that Bronx would be jealous of Gary, they're crazy. You can tell by the way Rebekah looks at Bronx that they share something unbreakable.

"His divorce from Amanda was final last week. He said he's sad, but she was so upset at the finale that he knew he'd never be able to convince her that he and I were only friends."

"In her defense, not that I want to defend her, you and Gary seemed to have something going on. I thought for sure you were leaving Bronx at the end of the show."

Smiling, Rebekah glances at Bronx. They both laugh.

"Should we tell her?" she asks, and he shrugs.

"Tell me what?" I ask, eager to know their secret. "Are you pregnant?" I'm sitting on the edge of my seat waiting.

Rebekah laughs. "No, and we're not trying."

"We are practicing though," Bronx says, waggling his eyebrows.

"The whole thing with Gary was a set-up from the producers. They didn't like the way Amanda was pawing after Josh. They found me through Gary's contacts and found out that I had recently married Bronx."

"The offer was something we couldn't give up."

"Give up what offer?" Josh comes back, followed by Rob. As soon as he sits down next to me, his arm is draped over my shoulder and he gives me a kiss.

"Get a room," Rob bellows out, causing us all to laugh.

"Bronx and Rebekah were telling me about Gary. They found Rebekah when Amanda started pissing the producers off. It was dumb luck that she was married to Bronx. Made everything perfect for the producers to send them in."

"Fuckers," Josh mutters. Everyone laughs except for Rebekah and me. The guys all have experience with shitty producers. I don't, but I'm sure that's about to change. I'm dreading what's upcoming. The thought of having the cameras following me around for six weeks, until Josh and I disappear behind the door of the honeymoon suite, is really stressful. The only bright spot, aside from marrying Josh again, is that my mother will be here soon. She's going to help us plan our dream wedding. It's not just mine, but Josh's as well, and I can't wait to marry him again.

"Barry is a snake," Bronx adds, increasing my anxiety toward the new show.

"Have they named your show?" Rebekah asks, moving closer to Bronx.

I shake my head and look at Josh, wondering if I missed something in the paperwork.

"No, I don't think so. I guess I never paid attention. I'm sure there's a name. And only half of the show will be live. At first I thought all six weeks, but it's only the last three."

"You guys are lucky. I want to go to Hawaii," Rebekah says.

I give Josh a knowing look before turning back to Bronx and Rebekah.

"Well one of the reasons you're here tonight is so I can ask if you want to be a bridesmaid?"

"Seriously?" she asks, as her legs start bouncing up and down.

"Yes, of course. We've grown close and I want to include you, Rebekah."

"Yes! I'd love to." We both stand and give each other a hug. When she sits back down, Bronx pulls her into his arms.

"My turn," Josh says. "Bronx, you and I may never be best friends, but you care for my wife and were there to make sure I saw the bigger picture. What do you say, are you up for being a groomsman?"

Bronx smiles so bright you'd think it's Christmas. "Yeah, man, I'm totally in." The guys don't hug, but they shake and clap hands and that seems to be enough for them.

"I'm going to start cooking," Josh says, taking the guys with him. I like that he's left Rebekah and me alone, because it gives us a chance to talk.

"So, how did Jules take the news?"

I shake my head. "I don't know. I half expected her to call Josh and claim the test was wrong, but she hasn't."

"That doesn't mean she won't."

"I know, and that's what I'm afraid of. What if she shows up during filming or somehow finds out the location of the wedding?"

"I won't let her ruin your wedding, Joey, don't worry."

I smile, knowing that I've found a friend for life in Rebekah.

"Crap, I'll be right back," I say when I hear the house phone ring. Josh and I thought about only using our cell phones, but we turn them off when we're home and I didn't want my parents not to be able to get a hold of us.

"Hello?"

"Mrs. Wilson, this is AJ from security. There's a woman here named Nina Springer."

"I'm sorry, but I don't know her. Please tell her we're not interested." I can hear AJ in the background talking to the woman. She's screeching and sounds very flamboyant.

"Ma'am, she says that she's Mr. Wilson's mother."

"I'm sorry, what?"

AJ repeats himself and she gets louder. "Um, hold on." After setting the phone down, I make my way back outside. Josh and the guys are laughing near the grill, enjoying themselves and drinking beer.

We've talked about his parents, but never discussed

having them at the house or even introducing me. He doesn't like them and feels they're going to taint our marriage. He's trying to be better.

He is better.

"Hey, babe," I say loud enough for him to hear me from the house.

"'Sup?" Turning, he gives me his million-dollar-panty-dropping smile.

"A woman, Nina Springer, is at the gate. She's claiming to be your mother."

Josh's face drops, along with his bottle of beer. The glass shatters as the beer coats the patio and I immediately know that our drama is far from over.

CHAPTER
twenty-four

Josh

I know Joey is standing there, watching me—along with Rob, Bronx, and now Rebekah—but I can't move. Today is supposed to be a good day ... no a great day, and yet the name that fell from my wife's lips has the power to ruin it all.

"Babe," Joey says again. I shake my head to bring myself back to reality. "The phone." She points over her shoulder toward the house and, more specifically, the table where we put our keys and where, currently, the house phone which has my mother waiting on the other end, is sitting patiently.

Swallowing hard, I look at Rob and Bronx for advice even though they have nothing to say. The only one here who has even come close to meeting my mother is Rob and I saved him from that agony.

"Babe," Joey says again, but this time she's tugging on my shirt. "Is that your mom?"

Letting out a huge breath, I run my hand through my hair. "Yeah it is, but I haven't told her where we live. I don't know how she found us."

"Okay, well she's on the phone. What do you want me to tell security?"

"Shit," I mutter, knowing full well that I can't send my mother away and thankful we don't have any of our spare bedrooms except for one available.

"Rob, go in the room by the garage and mess up the bed or something. I'm not letting my mom stay here."

I walk into the house with Rob and Joey on my heels. Joey is standing next to me when I pick up the phone. Closing my eyes, I pinch the bridge of my nose.

"You can let her in," I tell the guard.

"Sure thing, Mr. Wilson." He hangs up, sealing my fate. I lean against the table and inhale and exhale deeply, trying to calm my nerves.

"Is she that bad?" Joey rubs my shoulder, and while her touch usually calms me, it's not doing much to push my anxiety away.

I nod.

"If we handled Jules, this should be easy, right?"

"She's like Jules on crack," I groan.

"Oh."

Pulling Joey into my arms, I hold her as tightly as I can until the doorbell rings. Rob walks by, muttering something as he heads back outside.

"My parents don't know about you, unless they watched the show. I meant to tell them, but you'll see why I didn't once you meet her. My father is just as bad, but in a different way. All they want is money, or the fame that goes with being 'Joshua Wilson's' parents. I can't remember how many times they've been remarried, but I know it's over five."

"You told me in the house."

"Right." I nod, taking her hand in mine. We walk the few steps to the front door. "Oh, and she wears nothing but gold and diamonds. They're mostly fake, but she doesn't care.

God you're beautiful," I tell her before I kiss her.

Joey shocks me by reaching for the door. She swings it open as I stand behind her. My mother is looking away until she hears the door and turns slowly, taking in Joey before her eyes rise to meet mine.

"Did she sign a pre-nup?" My mother doesn't wait to be invited in. No, she brushes past Joey, bumping into her as if she's not standing right there.

I chuckle bitterly to myself and shake my head. Some things never change.

"Are you stupid? Is that how I raised you?" She holds her arm out toward us, indicating to the shawl draped over it, and eyes Joey.

"She's not your maid, Mother."

She scoffs. "I'm her mother-in-law."

"Only on paper," I say, hoping to remind her of where she stands in my life. It's a shame, but not uncommon, for parents of actors to act like this. They have expectations that aren't often met and expect to control every aspect of their child's life. I think it kills my mother that she's never been in control of my money.

"Well on paper I am everything to you." My mother eyes me defiantly and I find it comical.

Joey leans into me for moral support—or maybe to remind me that if I kill my mother I will no longer know what it feels like to have Joey touch me, given that I'll be behind bars for murder.

"To answer your question, no I'm not stupid, and considering you didn't raise me I think I'll leave that question alone. As for what's on paper, you're no longer the beneficiary on any of my accounts, Joey is and that isn't going to change any time soon." It feels damn good to say that to her and watch her face morph into something very few have seen.

"What about your father?"

I can't help but laugh at the absurdity of her question.

Always trying to one up him, or telling me that if I do something for him I have to do it for her.

"He's not either. Now tell me, who can I thank for your unfortunate arrival?"

"Josh," Joey chides. Even after the backhanded comment my mother made about her, she's still wants me to be nice. Unfortunately, I don't care enough about my mother's feelings to really give a shit.

"Yes, maybe you should listen to your wife about how you speak to me."

"Give my wife an hour and she'll be saying the same thing. So again, how did you find out where I live and what do you want?"

Instead of answering, she snubs her nose and walks into the house. I can't imagine what she's thinking right now. This house, by far, is nicer than anything she's ever owned. Each marriage for her has been about social status and class. Each new husband has to have a bigger bank account than the last or he has to be younger with an influx of money coming in.

"Mother." My tone is a warning, letting her know that I'm not going to continue to play this game with her.

"My daughter-in-law called me."

I look at Joey, who blanches and shakes her head.

"Joey did no such thing. She didn't even know your name until security called to let us know you were at the gate, so try again."

"I don't mean *her*," my mother sneers as she points toward Joey. "My sweet Jules, she called all upset that you were cheating on her and that you left her pregnant and alone."

I groan loudly, wondering when the hell my life is going to be somewhat normal for one day. That is all I want. One day where I don't have to hear about Jules.

"I don't even know where to start with this bullshit, Mother. First of all, you've never met Jules so you don't even know what she's like. Second, Jules and I were not together when I married Joey, not that it's any of your business. Third, while she's pregnant, the baby is not mine and I have the proof." I take a deep breath and Joey places her hand on my back, rubbing smoothly. "If you're concerned about Jules, I suggest you go to her place and spend some time with her. I'm sure you guys can bond over the antics you both use to get men."

She waves her hand as if she's dismissing me. "But you're my son, clearly you want me to spend time with you. Besides, you were raised better then this. You love Jules. You should be there for her. It shouldn't matter that the baby isn't yours."

Once again I find myself pinching the bridge of my nose. I have no doubt Bronx, Rob, and Rebekah are laughing at my expense as they listen to my mother. The only thing that would make this moment even better is if Matt and Jules show up. My life is turning into a freaking circus.

I'm trying to come up with a response that doesn't hurt her feelings, not that I care. I know I should be excited that she's here, but her intentions aren't pure.

"You know what, Mother—"

Joey interrupts me. "We love for you to visit. You're more than welcome to stay for dinner as well," Joey answers for me. I want to scream because she invited her for dinner, but she did the same for Jules. Maybe I should remind her that her good faith intentions toward Jules came back to bite us in the ass. I'll be sure not to let my mother wander around my house unsupervised. I wouldn't put it past her to pocket something she thinks has value.

"Yes, that will be fine. Would you mind showing me to my room? I'm exhausted from traveling and need to freshen up."

"Um …" Joey looks at up at me, her eyes full of worry.

"We just moved in and our spare bedroom is already occupied by Rob. You'll have to find someplace else to stay."

The shocked and hurt look on her face doesn't bother me even though it should. I don't care if we had all the rooms made up, I wouldn't let her stay here. She never had time for me when I was growing up, I don't know why I have to bend over backwards for her now.

"Well, I'll be."

"You should've called first. I could've saved you the drive up the hill if I knew you were in town. I'm sure there are vacancies somewhere."

She brushes me off again and heads toward the patio. I have no doubt she'll start drinking, forcing the issue that she won't be able to drive later.

"So help me—"

"It'll be fine, Josh." Joey wraps her arms around my waist. "Remember, I love you and there isn't anything she can say or do that is going to change that. And those people out there, they're our friends, not Jules', so even if your mother starts spouting crap about her they'll shut her down. She's outnumbered here."

"She shouldn't even be here."

"You're right, she shouldn't, but clearly Jules is grasping at anything to keep you in her life. I feel sorry for her, honestly."

"Me too."

I kiss Joey lightly, wishing that we were the only ones in our house. "I'm sorry she's here," I tell her, looking into her eyes. She smiles softly and that's enough to make things okay.

"We'll deal. It's what we do best."

"Yeah, but I'm tired of dealing. I'm honestly surprised you haven't left me yet with all this drama surrounding me."

"Ha," she says, laughing. "Next week when the cameras start following us around you can remind me why I'm still with you."

I gently tug on her ponytail. "You're getting the wedding of your dreams and you don't have to lift a finger. In my opinion, that should make me the best husband ever."

Joey rolls her eyes and laughs. "Come on, we have company that we have to entertain." She drags me outside even though I come willingly. When we get out there, everyone is sitting around the table, about to eat.

"Oh, I have stuff in the refrigerator," Joey says. Rebekah stands and offers to help. I want to run back into the house, but Rob and Bronx look at me like they need to be saved. Reluctantly, I sit down next to my mother.

"You have a very nice house here."

"Thank you," I say, honestly. The compliment is unexpected, but I'll take it.

"Does she work and pay rent or does she just clean and give you sex?"

Bronx spits his beer out all over the table and starts coughing. Rob pats his back and any ounce of compassion I had for this women is now gone. The gasp coming from my right is from Joey, who heard everything.

"Actually, Joey owns the house." Rebekah puts a bowl of potato salad down on the table. "She lets Josh live here."

"Excuse me?" my mother says.

I look to Rebekah who smirks.

"In case you didn't know, Joey is royalty as far as us Americans go."

"How so?"

I roll my eyes at how my mother's demeanor has changed suddenly.

"Well, I don't know if I should really divulge Joey's financial status. I mean that is really for her, you know, if she wants to tell you *who* exactly she is."

I glance quickly at Joey, who is hanging her head. It's only by chance that I see her laughing.

"Well, Josephine, what is it that you do?"

"Joey, her name is Joey," I tell my mother.

"Surely it's short for something more professional."

"Yeah, no, it's my name," Joey says. "As for what I do, I

sign up for reality television shows and marry rich actors." Joey shrugs while the rest of the table breaks out in laughter, except my mother narrows her eyes at Rebekah and I know that her wrath is going to be entertaining.

CHAPTER
twenty-five

Joey

I pace the floor, waiting for my mom to arrive. I wanted to go and pick her up, but Josh said that with the cameras already following me, it'd be a shit storm of media attention that I don't want or need. When I complained, he laughed and told me to get used to it.

"You might as well sit down," he calls to me from the living room.

"She might be here soon."

"Babe." His voice is right behind me and his hands are now on my shoulders. Sighing, I lean my head back into him. The small amount of anxiety I've been feeling is starting to dissipate. "She just landed. Give them time to get here. Traffic is a bitch right now."

Behind us I hear someone grumble about having to edit his language. For the past three days the cameras have been on us. We have granted them access to every part of our lives, except for what happens in our bedroom and bathroom. If people want to see what I'm eating for breakfast each morning or how Josh lounges on the couch, they'll get to. Nothing is off limits. The other condition we placed on the production crew was that we wouldn't allow cameras to be mounted in the home so if they wanted to film us, it had to be a live action crew and that means no nighttime filming. The last thing I wanted was to wake in the middle of the night and stumble into a tripod or trip over a crowd. When the lights go out, they go home. Home being the camper that is currently parked in our driveway.

Some may ask why I agreed to such an intrusive invasion of privacy and I wish the answer were simple. It's not. In the end, it came down to money.

When I returned from my three-day hiatus, Josh sat me down and explained the contract and everything that it entailed. Mostly it would be the same, except they wanted to pay us and the pay was negotiable. The starting price tag was one million dollars to follow us around, film our lives while we got ready for our wedding, and to have the exclusive rights to film our wedding and reception. I was ready to sign because it's what Josh wanted. For him the price wasn't enough, and when he called Barry asking for more, I thought he'd tell us to take a hike, but he came back with a few more zeroes on the proposed figure and that was enough for Josh. To think that someone is paying us millions of dollars for exclusive rights to our wedding is crazy.

"I'm just anxious to see her, that's all."

"I know, me too." Since our trip, Josh and my parents have grown very close and I honestly couldn't have asked for anything better. Although I do wish my mother hadn't asked for Josh's underwear size, even if she's shopping early for Christmas and buying him things for his stocking. There are some things a mother-in-law doesn't need to know.

Speaking of mothers-in-law, mine is still in town, but holed up at a hotel somewhere. There was a long, drawn out battle on why she couldn't stay here that ended with Josh suggesting she stay at the Beverly Hills hotel. She loved that idea until he told her he'd only pay for one night. He also failed to mention that my mother would be arriving soon and that the guest bedroom was for her. I know once Nina finds out she'll be upset. I don't think it'll be because my mother is here, or the fact that Nina isn't spending time with Josh, it'll be because she's not staying in our house so her social status as Josh's mother isn't getting the boost she wants.

Once Nina got wind that Josh and I were doing another stint on reality television she insisted on staying, stating she wanted to help with the wedding. That night I cried myself to sleep wondering what sort of nightmare my wedding was going to turn into now that she was around. I couldn't very well tell her no, but I didn't wholeheartedly agree either.

Josh finally pulls me toward the couch, bringing me to his chest as we sit down. The cameras move into position to record everything we do. I want to flip them off and maybe even stick my tongue out at them, but I promised that I would be polite. Josh turns the TV on for some background noise, but it doesn't do anything to calm me down. I miss my mom and I want her here, now.

"I should've gone to get her."

"The media would've been all up in your face, Joey. These guys here would've been there, alerting the paparazzi and your mother would've been subjected to a shit storm."

"Mark the time," someone says, causing me to laugh.

"You know, you won't be able to curse at our ceremony because it'll be live."

"Hmm, maybe I'll convince Barry to have a ten second delay because you know I won't be able to hold back once I see you walking down the aisle."

Yes, this is why we're going through all the painstaking rigmarole of having a wedding—to see me walk down the aisle. I get it. I see his point, but we've been married for months now and nothing is going to change that.

My mom and I will be meeting with the designer of my dress later today. When Josh told me what he did, calling the designer for help, I couldn't believe it. I know he loves me, but to do that really showed how much. The dress I had bought in Alabama was something I fell in love with, but this new one will be different. Jules ruined the other one for me. It's funny to think about everything she's done and the dress was the only thing she could actually ruin. If anything, she made the love Josh and I share even stronger.

"She's here," Josh whispers into my ear, his whiskers brushing lightly against my cheek. I stir and stretch my arms.

"I fell asleep."

"Yep you did. I think the camera crew appreciated it because they took a break. It's not much fun watching me watch TV while you're nestled in my arms, snoring."

My mouth drops open. "I was not!"

"You were and it was cute." He kisses my nose and helps me up. I run my fingers through my hair to straighten it out. Josh assures me I look decent and deep down I know I should run into the bathroom to make sure, but my front door is opening and my mother is walking in.

"Mom," I say as my voice cracks. She drops her bags and holds her arms out for me. I don't care if I saw her recently. I don't care if she's crazy and neurotic, she's my mother and I love her. "I'm so happy you're here."

"Me too, sweetie."

Once I let go of her, she's in Josh's arms. The cameraman moves to get a better angle and for once I'm grateful that they're here because if his mother could see the expression on his face when he hugs my mother, maybe she'd understand that she screwed up and try to change her ways. It's a small hope, but one I have nonetheless.

"Let's show you around."

I take my mom's hand and start the tour. Right off I show her the bathroom that everyone uses and then bring her into the dining room.

"Joey, you have no walls."

The windows are pulled back, letting the warm California sun into the home and brightening the massive space that makes up our dining and living room.

"We close them at night," I assure her.

"And this fireplace." Her hand trails along the brick until she walks to the other side. "Oh my, this home is lovely."

She can say it, it's freaking gorgeous. I pinch myself daily wondering how I got so lucky. That answer just wrapped his arms around me, kissing me on my neck.

We watch as my mom steps outside—sometimes watching people look around is better than giving them the tour.

"How do you leave for work everyday?" she asks Josh, who laughs.

"Believe me, it's not the house that makes it hard to leave." I don't know what sort of face he makes at her, but she covers her heart with one hand, while fanning herself with the other. I can't say I blame her, I often have to do that around Josh.

After showing her the office—which is currently an editing room for the production crew—we take her into the kitchen. "This is the kitchen and our breakfast nook."

"Joey, your nook is bigger than my kitchen." She's exaggerating, but yes it's huge and far too much space for Josh and me.

"This is the mudroom, laundry room, and direct access to the garage and this will be your bedroom." Josh opens the door and lets her walk in. It isn't anything magnificent, but the view of the hills is breathtaking. We're up high enough that we overlook most of the valley.

"And you have a private bathroom," Josh adds.

"And I feel like I'm far enough removed that I won't hear you two having a little fun at night."

191

"Mother," I chide and slyly motion over my shoulder at the camera.

She shrugs. "It's not like I don't know you guys have sex … you were at my house for God's sake."

I'm officially mortified. Not only were Josh and I not discreet enough when we were at their house, but she's now blasted it all over the airwaves because you know they won't edit this part out.

My husband is no help as he stands here, laughing. "Come on, Ava, let me show you the rest of the house."

She follows Josh down the hall, stopping in each of the rooms. When we get to the second to the last room, he refers to it as the nursery. Her eyes go wide and her smile falls as I shake my head.

"Not yet," he says, "but we're working on it." I know her and my father will make amazing grandparents and I'm willing to bet they move here, although I'd want to visit them often. I'd rather my children be able to grow up with land around them and a place to play instead of the concrete yard. We both know playing out front where we have a tiny bit of grass will never fly.

The last stop on the tour is our bedroom and the cameras aren't allowed in there. After shutting the door, I lean up against it. "Finally, some privacy," I say to both of them.

"Does it get annoying?"

"Yes," I tell her. "It's different from when we were in the house, though. Those cameras were all around us, but suspended. Never up in your face, but still there and you were never able escape to them unless you won a competition and you were given access to the master suite."

"You'll get used to them, Ava." Josh stands, leaning up against the wall that opens to the outside.

"Do you ever fall asleep with that wall missing?"

"Often. Sometimes we get a nice breeze and if I don't fall asleep outside, I definitely do on that bed. It's the most comfortable thing I've ever slept in."

Mom continues to survey the room, including the bathroom, closets, and exercise room that only has a treadmill.

"Well, Josh, I have to say, I'm thoroughly impressed with your house."

"Our house," he corrects. "Joey and I bought it together. It may have been my money that paid for it, but with what she's earning from the show, it more than covers her half. Not that I'm asking her to pay. Everything I have is hers."

I go to him and easily fall into his arms.

"Joey, I don't know how you keep any clothes on with him around. I'd be walking around naked and falling at his feet every time he opened his mouth."

Josh blushes and so do I but not in the way that counts.

"Mother!"

"Eh." She shrugs and walks out of the room, running right into the cameraman before I can stop her.

I'm left with no choice but to follow her out. We have an appointment with my designer and I need to warn her about Nina … although, considering my mom's penchant for embarrassing me in front of the cameras maybe I'll let Nina introduce herself.

CHAPTER
twenty-six

Josh

Right now my favorite time of the day is at night, or any time I can escape behind my closed bedroom door. It's the only time when the cameras aren't watching mine, or our, every move. The producers have even started asking us questions to incite a conversation or induce drama when we don't need it. I'm starting to think this was a bad idea, but then I remember the bigger picture and the pay out at the end.

If Joey were to use a wedding planner or plan our wedding herself, she'd be stressed. Not that she isn't now, but it would be more amplified because she'd worry about money. She doesn't understand that I'd move Heaven and Earth to give her the wedding of her dreams.

It's been almost two weeks since production started and, quite frankly, that's nine days too long. I've heard them complain that we're boring, mundane, and lacking the drama needed to bring in the viewers. On the inside I was smiling because that is the best way to be in my opinion. If they wanted the drama maybe they should've started when Jules was hanging around. There was plenty of it to go around.

Joey stirs in her sleep. Her head is rested on my chest with her arm draped across my stomach and I'm wide-awake, wondering how I got here. I'm not having cold feet or even second-guessing anything, I'm only having a hard time coming to grips with how everything changed. One drunken night and I signed my name on a contract that's changing my life.

I used to think my life made sense until I met Joey, then what I thought I wanted went out the door. She makes everything seem so simple when my life was nothing but a complicated mess.

The house phone rings, jolting Joey in my arms. My hand runs smoothly down her arm, trying to lull her back to sleep. It's too late for guests and honestly I'm surprised that security would call this late. I close my eyes once the ringing stops and try to get some shut-eye. Tomorrow … well, actually today, is going to be a long but fun day. We're getting fitted for our tuxedos and Joey's dad is arriving. I'm excited that he'll be here before we leave for Hawaii even if he'll be bored.

When the phone rings again I jump up out of bed and rush down the hall. It's a good thing the cameramen are sleeping or they'd have a nice shot of me in my underwear right now.

"Hello," I bark into the receiver, not worrying about the person on the other end.

"Hi, I'm looking for Joshua Wilson."

"This is Joshua, who is this?"

"My name is Edna and I'm calling from Cedars-Sinai to let you know that Jules Maxwell is in labor and she's asking for you."

I pinch the bridge of my nose, a new habit that I've picked up recently from being on set with my last film, and sigh. "I'm not the baby's father," I tell the nurse. "She needs to call someone else."

"She did, Mr. Wilson, and no one has shown up."

"I'm sorry, but I won't be there either." I hang up before she can try and talk me into doing something I don't want to do. Being there for Jules is the last thing I want. It's the last thing Joey and I need. We are only a few of weeks away from getting married and we should be focusing on us, not her.

"Hey," Joey says as I come back into the bedroom. "Who was that?"

"A nurse from Cedars. Jules is in labor and she called to let me know."

"Why?"

I crawl back into bed, but sit up against the headboard. My mind is racing a mile a minute and I know that sleep won't be coming for me anytime soon.

"Because no one has shown up for her."

"She's alone?"

I shrug. "I didn't ask."

Joey snuggles into my side, making sure to keep the sheet up over her bare breasts.

"We should go, Josh."

"No, we shouldn't."

"If the baby was yours, you'd be there. I would, too, even though I wouldn't be welcome, but she wouldn't be alone."

Joey has a good heart. It doesn't matter what people are saying about her, and in this case, I mean Jules and my mother, all she sees is that a woman is alone and going through something important and probably traumatic.

"Joey, if we go, she'll think I'm there because I love her."

She sits up and keeps a tight grip on the sheet, preventing me from seeing her breasts. Jules isn't even here and she's cock blocking me right now.

"I can imagine that having a baby is scary, but being alone or having to only depend on the hospital staff to help you is probably really freaking her out. Knowing that a friend is waiting for her in the waiting room will soothe her a little."

"Joey," I say, closing my eyes, "this isn't a good idea."

"Nothing concerning Jules is a good idea," she replies, hopping off the bed. She disappears into her closet and when she comes out, she's dressed in sweats and a T-shirt, and is in the process of piling her hair on top of her head.

"I'm going."

"Joey," I whine, throwing the covers off my legs. "This is a mistake."

Cupping my face with her hands, she gazes into my eyes. I know she sees nothing but torment in them. "You'll feel better knowing you were there, I promise. There was a time in your life when you loved her and I know she's done a lot to ruin everything you guys had, but right now she's scared and she called the one person she knows won't come to her aid. She's desperate, Josh, she has no one else."

Deep down I know that Joey is right and if I hadn't pushed for the paternity test I'd be at the hospital right now waiting for Jules to give birth. I kiss Joey and sidestep her to get dressed. When I come out, she's in the kitchen talking to her mom.

"Morning, honey," Ava says, handing me a travel mug of coffee.

"Thank you."

"I'll call you as soon as we know something." Joey kisses her mom and we make our way to the car. We'll have enough time to get out of the garage and down the road before the production realizes the noise they can hear is Joey and I leaving.

"Barry is going to be pissed," I say, turning out of our community and heading down the hill toward the hospital. At night Hollywood is gorgeous and I've always loved it. The nightlife is still bustling, creating a glow.

"It's none of his business."

"No, but Jules will see this as a missed opportunity to sell her story."

Joey doesn't say anything, but I suspect she's rolling her eyes. She wants to see the good in everyone even when they don't deserve it.

"I can guarantee you that *People* magazine will be there as soon as she delivers."

"Josh …"

"Joey, I know you want to believe she'll change after giving birth, but I doubt it. The baby will be an accessory until the novelty wears off and then it will be a burden. I know her better than most. She's never going to change."

We're silent the rest of the way to the hospital and when we pull in I'm thankful that the media isn't outside waiting. I've never come out and publicly denied Jules' baby, but I haven't admitted it either. Most people are going to assume I'm the father and while that bothers me, Blaze felt that doing damage to her professional career wasn't a smart move on my part. As long as Joey and her parents know the truth, that's all that matters.

Joey leads us to the desk and asks where we can find Jules.

"I'm sorry, we don't have anyone registered by that name," she tells us.

"Please try Juanita Madonno."

The nurse starts typing again and Joey looks at me. With a shrug, I start walking toward the room number the nurse blurted out.

"Juanita? Is that her alias?"

"No, that's her name. Jules is her stage name."

"Is Joshua Wilson a stage name and I'm really married to someone else?" she asks as we press the buzzer to be let into maternity.

"Nope, Joshua Wilson is who I am."

"Phew," she says, wiping her forehead. I laugh out loud

and a nurse behind the desk glares at me. When we find Jules' room, Joey tells me she'll wait by the door.

I knock and step in. The second Jules sees me, her face lights up. She reaches for me, but I stay, standing against the wall.

"You came."

I shake my head. "I didn't want to, but Joey made me … she made us."

"She's here?" Her tone is snarky.

"Out in the hall."

"Why? Why couldn't you leave her at home?" Jules flops back on her bed and cries out, I'm assuming she's having a contraction or whatever they are. "Why, Josh?"

"Because she's my wife, Jules. And for whatever reason she wanted to be here for you when I wanted to go back to sleep. My wife thought you needed a friend."

A nurse comes in to soothe Jules. I feel bad, but refuse to move from the wall. "Are you the father?"

"No, I'm not," I say, sternly.

The nurse never makes eye contact with me. "It's time, Jules."

"Will you stay while I give birth? I need you, Josh."

Shaking my head, I direct my gaze at the ground. "No, this is something I need to experience with my wife the first time. I'll be out in the hall when you're done."

She starts crying, but it's not enough to pull me toward her. I step outside and pull Joey to me. "This was a mistake."

"I heard what she said."

"I told you, Joey. She doesn't care if we're married. She's delusional and can't accept that I'm not part of her life anymore. Can we leave? Please." Even though I told Jules I'd be out in the hall, I know that there is no part of me that wants to be here. I *can't* be here, not anymore. The doormat I've been when it comes to Jules Maxwell has to stop and now seems to be as a good time as any.

"I'm sorry, I thought in her condition she'd want a friend."

"She wants me and the feelings aren't mutual. She's never going to change."

Joey wipes some tears, and for the life of me I can't understand why she's crying. Taking her under my arm, I escort her out of the hospital as fast as I can.

"You're a good person, Joey, but I need you to develop some thicker skin for this world we're in. Don't take everyone at face value and don't assume they're not trying to stab you in the back," I tell her as soon as we get in the car. I've been burnt by one too many snakes in this industry and I don't want to see Joey go through the same thing.

"I just thought—"

"You know," I say, taking her hand in mine. "With anyone else, they would've welcomed us being there for them, but not with her. She has tunnel vision when it comes to what she wants."

With a sigh, Joey leans back in her seat. "I suppose I ought to watch for her trying to steal my husband," she says, squeezing my hand.

"Not where I'm concerned." I bring her hand up and kiss it. "As far as I'm concerned you're the one for me and the only one I see in my life."

She turns her head and smiles.

By the time we get home, the sun is almost peaking out over the horizon. "Let's get some sleep before your dad arrives. Us guys have a busy day."

"You're trying on tuxedos." She points out as she undresses down to nothing and crawls into bed.

"Mhm," I say, palming my already growing erection. "And drinking, hitting the golf course, and planning my stag party." I pull the covers back, causing her to giggle. Grabbing a hold of her ankles, I pull her to me before dropping my shorts onto the floor. "Look at that." I palm my cock, rubbing it against her.

"What? I don't feel anything." She's a little vixen teasing me like this.

"You will in a second, babe." I plunge into her, making sure she feels every single inch of what I'm about to give to her.

CHAPTER
twenty-seven

Joey

The sweet smell of salt water fills the air. The waves rush to the shore while birds fly above trying to find their breakfast. I'm the only one on the beach, but that will change once the guests at the resort start waking up. The employees will be out, setting up umbrellas for shade, kids will be splashing in the sea, and surfers, boats, and people who plan to swim will be frolicking in the water.

Last night I had to kiss Josh good-bye. I've had to do it before, but this time it was different. He'd be going to a suite with Rob while I went to one with my parents. We won't see each other until later this evening when I walk down the wooden dock that will be laid out for me. I teased him and asked why he didn't want to stay the night with his mother and step father, or even his father and brand new step mom.

Nina wasted no time informing Josh's dad about our new house in the hills, the reality show, and our destination wedding. And like her, he showed up, but did one better than her and brought Josh's shiny new step mom. By shiny I mean very plastic and very young. It took about twenty minutes of her touching his arm before I had enough of her and gave them directions to the nearest hotel. Of course that wasn't good enough for his father and he demanded one of the rooms be made up for them.

Demanded.

I told him I'd get right on it. The rooms are still bare and as long as his parents are in town they'll remain that way. What really sucks is that they con Josh out of money. I don't like it, but it's not my place to say anything. I know what's his is mine and all that, but it doesn't seem right. I'm not the one earning what he's spending on their hotel rooms. The one thing he did do, which I laughed about for hours, is offer them a suite to share at a fairly nice hotel, or separate rooms at a cheaper one. Shockingly they took the cheaper one.

Behind me, the cameraman is filming. Every now and again he gets up and walks around to get me face on. He's asking questions, trying to get me to open up about today and how I feel.

"It's funny," I tell him. "Josh and I have been married eight months, you would think any nerves I have would be gone."

"But they're not?"

"No. I think they're stronger than ever because now I know what to expect. Before I had no expectations. I thought the man I matched with wouldn't haven't anything in common with me or he'd be someone I never thought I'd see myself with."

"You mean ugly?"

"No, I didn't say that." I keep my gaze focused on the ocean. You have to be careful what you say, or how you react around the camera because the smallest things get blown out of proportion. Blaze PR has me on all the social media sites, and while I do have access and can post, I rarely respond to anything. People can be intrusive and because you're a

203

public persona they feel you have to answer every question they throw at you. Ask me what I ate for breakfast and I'll tell you. Ask me what Josh wears to bed or how many times we have sex and I'll ignore you.

"Are you excited for today?"

"I am."

The theme is mermaid with aqua blues, seashells, and sand candles. We figured if we were getting married at the beach it might as well be beach themed. The wooden dock or aisle was my mother's idea so I could wear heels. Nina's idea was to ask the wedding guests to bring money as gifts. I have no doubt in my mind that if we did that we would never see the checks. Aside from a few suggestions from her, everything has been what Josh and I want, with input from my mom.

My toes dig into the sand, wiggling their way deeper and deeper until my ankles are covered. I thought it would be cold this early in the morning, but it's not. I like being out here this early by myself. It gives me time to think even with the camera pointed at me.

My mom, Rebekah, Nina, and I will have breakfast together before going to the spa where my day starts with a massage, followed by a mani/pedi treatment, and finally hair and nails. My hair is going to be curled and off to the side with a seashell barrette I found at a mall kiosk. It was a lucky find and as soon as I saw it I knew I needed it for today.

I had hoped Millie would come to the wedding, but being very pregnant and flying over the Pacific Ocean is highly frowned upon. Cole and her are still married, which means they'll likely get the house on our one-year anniversary, but they're not together. They live in separate states and Cole comes to visit her.

She took my advice and started looking into his mother and found that she's a dirty crook. Their relationship is different. For the longest time Millie wanted him back and when he finally pulled his head out of his ass, her feelings had long changed because of the resentment she's been harboring. I feel bad for her. In a way her relationship is as twisted as Jules wanted mine and Josh's to be.

Out of all of us I thought for sure Millie and Cole would be the ones to make it. I pretty much knew Gary and Amanda would end, and as far as Josh and I, I had hope.

Turns out that hope is all I needed.

My legs feel wobbly and my steps tentative. I hate heels, but they're an evil necessity for this dress.

My dress …

I fell in love with the first one from the bridal boutique in Alabama, but when I met with the designer and she showed a sample of a champagne-colored gown similar to the one I had chosen, that's when I knew Jules had done me a favor. I'm still Cinderella, but the beadwork I have is now smooth, soft silk that shimmers in the light. I can run my hands over my bodice and not be afraid to pull or rip something. Josh and I can dance and he'll be able to touch me without snagging a bead or getting one caught on his cufflink.

Each step I take closer to my dad, brings back memories from the show, except now I can see. I'm not blindfolded. This time I'll see him standing at the end of the wooden aisle way, standing proud and looking dapper in his tux. His smile is bright and happy. I have no doubt he was like this before, but I don't have the proof. Now I do.

"Are you ready?"

I nod, probably too eagerly but I don't care. It feels like I'm marrying Josh for the first time.

"I am."

As if on cue the violins play the "Wedding March" over the crashing waves. My mom, Rebekah, and my cousins have already walked down the aisle. I'm the only one left.

Carefully stepping onto the wooden planks, I look at the pink rose petals my flower girl set out for me. My dad bends his arm at his elbow and offers it to me. Inhaling deeply, we walk toward the bend that will put my Josh right before me. Once I turn the corner, we'll see each other for the first time in eighteen long, painful hours.

"If it helps, he's nervous, too."

"I'm not nervous," I lie. I'm terrified, but it's reassuring to know that Josh is in fact waiting for me at the end of the aisle.

My dad turns the corner, slowly. My head is down and I hear gasps from our friends and family—this time I smile knowing that they're here for me and not because I'm marrying Joshua Wilson. To them he's just Josh. To me he's my future.

Slowly I lift my head, unable to keep the smile off my face. I'm so in love with the man who is standing a few feet from me that the only thing keeping me from running the rest of the way are the heels. I'd rather not end up in the hospital on my wedding day.

When our eyes meet I can feel the magnetic pull between us. He cocks his head to the side as a wide smile dances on his lips. He whispers something that I can't hear, but Rob laughs and shakes his head.

My father tugs on my arm, lurching me forward. One-step forward, then two, three, and four. I'm almost there. The justice of the peace steps up with his book in his hand and behind me everyone sits. Cameras move into place and mics are dangled above us since I refused to wear one with my dress.

"Welcome. I'm sure you're all happy to be here on this beautiful day. We've been very blessed with amazing weather and even more with a magnificent bride and groom.

"Who gives this woman to be with this man?"

"Her mother and I do, happily." My father kisses my

hand before placing it in Josh's. Much to my surprise he gives Josh a hug and pats him on the back.

"You're fucking gorgeous."

I blush and remember we're live. "Josh," I scold, but he laughs.

"I don't care. I told Barry we needed a delay."

He did, many times, but Barry insisted on being live and Josh cleaning up his language. Looks like Barry will be getting a fine.

Josh and I adjust and make sure we're standing on the blue taped X. We've rehearsed this part over and over again so we should know better.

"You really are beautiful."

"You're pretty handsome yourself."

"Joshua and Joey began their lives together in the most unheard of circumstances. Instead of following the age-old techniques of courtship, they married each other with blindfolds on, sight unseen. They didn't even know each other's names until they were husband and wife.

"Surely a marriage that starts like this is a hard road to travel, especially when you're forced to live and compete with other married couples. For Josh and Joey, love prevailed as millions of friends watched Joey chip away at the walls Josh put up. And when their time was up, Josh did it for real by proposing to his wife. He wanted to give her this." He spreads his arms out wide and I find myself looking around as well. The view is breathtaking and even the onlookers who are being held back by tape and security can only see two people standing here, but can enjoy the scenery.

"If you would join hands."

I turn and hand my mother my bouquet of peonies and roses. My bridal party is dressed in mermaid-style dresses that flare at the knee, not the ankle. I wanted them to enjoy the party later and not have to shuffle their feet. The light blue satin is perfect against the light brown sand and crystal blue ocean backdrop.

"Joshua, if you would please."

Clearing his throat, he squeezes my hands. We chose to write our own vows or speak from our hearts instead of using the traditional ones. We figured there's nothing traditional about us yet, so why start now.

"Joey, sometimes I find it hard to express what I'm feeling when it comes to you. Love doesn't seem like a strong enough word to fully grasp the way I feel or how you make me feel. Marrying you all those months ago was a game changer for me. You opened my eyes to a world that I never wanted anything to do with and showed me how easy it is to fall in step behind you. I can't promise you that I'll never do something stupid, or piss you off, but I can promise you this … I am going to love you for the rest of my days. I am going to do everything I can to make you smile, hear you laugh, and show you that you mean more to me than anything. I love you, Joey."

Everyone aws as I catch the tears pooling in my eyes. It's my turn and for a few weeks I have struggled with what I'm going to say. I thought I had it down until everything changed for me.

"Joshua Freaking Wilson," I start, causing everyone to laugh. "There aren't a lot of people here who don't know how infatuated I was with you. And yes, I say was because now that I know you I can easily say that reality is far better than what I made up in my head. The person I thought you were pales in comparison to the man you are. You're thoughtful, caring, and the most generous man I have ever loved. Every day with you has been a challenge and a blessing. I can't wait to love you tomorrow, the next day, and every moment in between. My love for you is only going to grow stronger with each passing day and I can't wait to see what our future holds. I love you, Josh. You're going to make an amazing father to our baby."

My teeth catch my lower lip as his mouth drops open and our family gasps. Only my mother and Rebekah know that I'm pregnant and behind me I can hear them giggling.

"Wh-what?" he sputters.

"I'm pregnant," I whisper for him. Telling the television audience was never my plan, but I figured it would be better than trying to hide it and dodging all the questions about my weight.

"You're kidding?"

Smiling, I shake my head.

"Holy fuck," he says, smashing his mouth down on mine. The justice of the peace is reminding him that he hasn't given him permission yet, but I don't think he cares. When we part, I'm breathless and wanting more.

"We're having a baby?"

"Yeah, we are."

"Ahem, do you think we could finish?"

"Oh right," Josh replies, stepping back slightly.

"Rings?" the JP says, sighing. Rob and my mom hand us our rings and the JP goes through his spiel. Josh kisses my ring after he places it on my finger.

"I suppose I can skip the 'do you' parts because it's clear that you do," the JP says, causing everyone to laugh. "By the power vested in me in the great state of Hawaii, I pronounce you once again, Mr. and Mrs. Wilson. You know what to do Josh, let her have it."

And he does!

epilogue

"What are you doing?"

Wrapping her hands around my waist from behind, Joey kisses my bare shoulder. I'm leaning against the doorjamb, watching. This is where I am every night about three a.m., waiting.

"I'm addicted."

"I know. Me too," she says, sighing. I maneuver my arm so Joey is nestled into my side, never taking my eyes off the white princess crib that sits in the middle of the room.

Jolie Hope is three months old and the most amazing achievement of my life. Not that I did anything other than help conceive her. Joey did it all. She did everything to nurture Jolie and bring her into this world. But I was there, every step of the way from prenatal yoga, childbirth classes, and now swim lessons.

After Joey told me, and subsequently the world, that she was pregnant instant fear set in about our swimming pool. I wanted to cover it while Joey suggested a fence. She won out, but the moment Jolie's doctor gave the okay that she could be in the water, I put her in and hired a lifeguard to come teach her. I know she's young and I'm probably wasting my money, but whatever, maybe I'm raising the next Olympian.

As I predicted, Barry was front and center with a contract ready for us to sign, but this time I put my foot down. I didn't want something like this broadcast for millions of people. I didn't want Joey judged if she decided to have a glass of wine at dinner, which her doctor said was perfectly fine. Truthfully, I wanted her growing belly to be for my eyes only. I didn't want viewers to see me cradling her stomach, whispering to my daughter or reading a bedtime story to her while Joey rubbed the spots that Jolie was kicking. I needed this to be private.

I also didn't want Jules anywhere near us and knew that if we were filming, she'd want to be front and center creating unneeded drama. I haven't seen her since the night in the hospital, when she was giving birth. She had a boy who she named Josh. If I could've sued her over that I probably would've, but at this point there isn't anything I can do. The speculation will always be there that I'm the baby's father, no matter how many times I deny it. It's been my speculation that Matt, my former agent, is the father, but it's my hunch. It's not like I can publicly say it's him without a lawsuit being brought against me.

Joey and I struggled with a name for Jolie. Many friends came out of the woodwork to offer suggestions, and while some were far reaching, I didn't want my daughter to grow up with a name like Cricket or Pilot. I wanted something normal and beautiful and Joey wanted Hope.

For Joey, the baby was tying us together in a way our vows and wedding rings couldn't. She said that for the first three months of our marriage, she lived off hope, hoping that I'd change my mind about a future. It paid off for her, for us.

We settled on Hope until I saw her. Everything changed after I held her. I knew Hope wasn't going to be the right name for her.

I wanted something that captured her beauty. She is the best parts of Joey and me … well, more so her mother, but I'm biased. I wanted our first born to have a connection to us so I suggested we call her Jo. As you can ascertain, Joey was not onboard and started looking up names while our daughter snuggled half on her mom's chest and half on mine, in the cramped hospital bed. I was doing the same and blurted out, "Jolie," and the meaning, "A pretty young woman."

"Jolie Hope," I whispered, gazing at my daughter and when I looked at my wife, she had a tear in her eye. "Jolie Hope Wilson," I said again, being rewarded with a kiss that at any other time would've led to other things.

Jolie tries to sleep through the night and when I say tries, it's mostly because I've woken her up by subtle touches or from me leaning on her crib. In a few days, I start filming another movie with the location being about an hour away. I'm going to be gone during most of her awake time and I'm not sure how I'm going to handle that. Asking Joey to bring her to set will be cumbersome and Jolie probably won't appreciate the long car ride.

"Let's go back to bed." Joey pushes me slightly toward our room and I barely budge.

"One more minute," I say.

Sighing, Joey shakes her head. "I'm getting naked, Mr. Wilson. I think you know what that means."

I watch her over my shoulder as she takes off her top. Her bra is still in place due to the fact that she's nursing, which honestly makes me a bit jealous of Jolie. One of my favorite times during the day is when she's nursing. I'll hold Joey, essentially making it so I'm holding both my girls and talk to Jolie, telling her I used to suck on her mom's nipples and ask her if I can have my job back. Being that she's only three months old I'm not scarring her for life … yet.

Groaning, I scrub my hand over my face before shutting Jolie's door. "You drive a hard bargain, woman." I close our door and strip down.

"I'm not bargaining. You're about to start filming and I have a feeling that you'll be tired when you get home. Jolie will surely take all your attention." She winks at me. I know she's kidding, but the possibility that she'd even think I wouldn't have time for her kills me.

Grabbing her ankle, I pull her toward the end of the bed. She squeals and tries to get away, but I'm faster than her.

"You'll always be number one to me, Joey."

"Mhm, I'm not so sure about that."

I hover over her, careful not to put any weight on her. In the beginning of her pregnancy nothing changed for us. If anything our sex lives increased, especially in her second trimester. But her third was another story. She was hot, I was filming, and if given the chance she'd sleep in the pool. I'd often come home to find her asleep with the blinds pulled on the windows, the air conditioner blasting and a fan directly on her. As much as I wanted her, I knew she was miserable and probably could do without my body heat so I did what any self-respecting man would do, I begged. Most of the time it worked, but there was about a month that it didn't and it killed me. I had to watch her walk about with her cute belly, big tits, and rocking body. It didn't matter that she was pregnant; my wife worked out, which benefited her during delivery and postpartum. She dropped the excess baby weight, except for a cute little pouch that I absolute adore because that is where she held my baby for so long, making her perfect.

I kiss her belly and cup her breast. "Can I play with them?" I ask, not wanting to hurt her. I know they're sensitive from breastfeeding.

"Yes." She pulls down her straps as my fingers reach for

213

the cups. Her boobs pop free and are held up by her bra, giving me the perfect opportunity to bring them close to my mouth. I lap at her nipples, alternating between the two. Joey arches, digging her fingers into my ass to push me closer to where she wants me. My already erect dick is bouncing with anticipation as he brushes against her pussy.

"Josh," she moans out my name.

"Patience." I want to take my time, but time is not on our side right now. Jolie is due for a feeding soon so I need to work fast and make sure Joey is completely sated. I sit back on my knees and pull her legs up. My mouth waters at the sight of her pussy. "Baby, are you wet for me?" I ask, sliding a finger between her lips. Her eyes close, she grips my arm, and moans again. "Always so ready for me," I murmur against her skin.

I love a horny Joey.

I flatten myself out along the bed and drop her legs around my shoulders. She calls out as my tongue comes in contact with her clit. Joey lifts her hips for friction against her clit while my fingers work her inside.

"Kiss me," she says, breathlessly. I do. Dropping her legs between my hips, I cocoon her in my arms and plunge my tongue into her mouth. She moans and kisses me back with fury. Her hand snakes between our bodies and she lines me up. All I have to do is push and I'm connected to her. I reach for the drawer on her nightstand and fumble around until my fingers come in contact with a condom. We're back to practicing safe sex due to her nursing and us not wanting another baby right away. I want to enjoy Jolie before we add another.

I've become a pro at putting on a condom while kissing her. It's a feat really and I know I should write an instruction manual on safe loving. Once it's secure, it's game on.

Joey cries out when I enter her. She bites her lower lip as I grab ahold of her tits. As much as I love watching them bounce as I fuck her, I know they get sore and the last thing I want to do is cause her any pain.

"Fuck, Joey." I slide in and out of her slowly, watching as my cock becomes one with her.

"Faster," she begs and I comply, gripping her hips to increase my thrusting. It's only a matter of seconds before I'm falling on top of her and pumping vigorously. "Oh, oh, oh, yes … shit," she bellows out, nails digging into my back.

I groan when I feel her walls start to tighten around me as my impending orgasm builds. "Joey, baby …"

She doesn't respond except by quivering beneath me. It's the best fucking feeling in the world, when her and I are like this. I come shortly after her, collapsing on top of her as Jolie's wail fills our room.

"Perfect timing," she says, out of breath.

"I'll get her." I dress quickly and make my way across the wall where my daughter cries out, not for me, but for her mother. It doesn't hurt my feelings because I know one day I'll be her hero. I look forward to the days where she dresses me up and invites me to her tea parties.

"Hi, my sweet girl." I look over the side of her crib and she whimpers. Tiny tears slide down her face. I wipe them and her cheek flinches telling me that she's ready for some boobie action. "I know, my pretty girl. I love Mommy's boobs, too."

Scooping her up, I take her over to her changing table. I'm a master at diapers and try to help Joey every chance I get, even with the unpleasant ones. Once I have her changed, she's nestled into my neck sucking on her hand and slobbering all over my shoulder.

"Look who I found." I turn her around so she can see Joey. Little squeals are emitted and her tiny feet kick. "It's the moo moo truck," I say, depositing her into Joey's waiting arms. Jolie latches on and begins suckling instantly. This is the part where most dads are left out, or roll over and go to sleep. Not me.

Sliding in behind Joey, I hold her in my arms, kissing her neck in between watching our daughter nurse. It's moments like these that make my life feel complete.

"People should be jealous of me." I trail my finger down Jolie's cheek and she smiles. Her eyes are the color of Joey's—light blue, but sometimes gray or green.

"Why's that?" Joey asks.

"Because I have the most gorgeous wife and legit the prettiest baby ever."

"Maybe we should bottle your sperm and sell it." Joey laughs, but I don't find it funny.

"Sorry, babe. My junk is strictly for you."

"That's the best answer." She leans back into my chest and continues to nurse Jolie. When she switches sides, so do I. I like watching them together, burning them into my memory.

"Thank you, Joey."

"For what?"

"For not giving up on me when it would've been so easy to do, for seeing me as more than an actor and making me believe in myself, in you, and in love. For giving me a chance when others tried to fuck it up for us. And most importantly, for making me a father. Jolie is the best gift I could've ever asked for."

Joey leans to the side and presses her lips against mine. I hold her there, cupping her cheek. When Jolie grunts, we both laugh and pull away.

"She's jealous."

I can't help but laugh. "You know," I say, flexing my arm. "I'm told I'm a catch."

Joey rolls her eyes. "Only in your twisted reality, Joshua Freaking Wilson … and in mine, too."

That's a compliment that I'll take to the bank!

the end!

acknowledgements

To my crew, as always, thank you for everything that you do to help bring each idea to life. You guys put up with a lot of harebrained ideas and I appreciate it. Amy, Audrey, Tammy and Veronica – you guys work so hard to make sure everyone knows about my stories, thank you.

The design team, Sarah and Emily, thank you for always being there!

Thank you, Melissa and Virginia, thank you for dropping everything and helping me out.

To my family – as always I appreciate everything you do.

about the author

Heidi is a New York Times and USA Today Bestselling author.

Originally from Portland, Oregon and raised in the Pacific Northwest, she now lives in picturesque Vermont, with her husband and two daughters. Also renting space in their home is an over-hyper Beagle/Jack Russell, Buttercup and a Highland Westie/Mini Schnauzer, JiLL and her brother, Racicot.

When she isn't writing one of the many stories planned for release, you'll find her sitting courtside during either daughter's basketball games.

Chapter **ONE**

Lara

"Crank, you stupid piece of donkey shit. Just two more miles, that's it. I promise to never starve you again!" I yelled, slamming my hands against the steering wheel. I turned the key one last time, but the damn thing just sputtered. Groaning, I closed my eyes and rested my head against the wheel.

My sister was busy working at the restaurant we owned, and my best friend was most likely busy with her new, dreamy, football-playing husband. I had no one to call. When had I become such a loser?

Huffing, I pulled a pair of shorts and a tank top out of my bag and stripped down. If I was going to walk two miles in the blistering heat, I wasn't going to do it wearing a blouse and pants. Already drenched in sweat, I got out of the car and winced as the sun beat down on my skin. There wasn't a single cloud to hide the unforgiving sun. Summer was brutal in North Carolina.

"This has to be payback for something," I whined,

trekking alongside the road. It was two o'clock in the afternoon, the worst time of day. Either everyone was at work, or at home, relaxing by their pools. I was never going to let my car get below a quarter of a tank again. Ever.

A couple of people honked their horns, but no one stopped. What ever happened to southern hospitality?

A rumble came up from behind and a muffled shout called out, "Lara!"

Jerking to a stop, my breath caught in my lungs. I was surprised he would even take the time to pull over for someone in need. Luke Collins was all about getting pussy, twenty-four-seven. And I hated the fact I'd ever had a crush on him. Granted, he had gotten much worse since losing Kate to Cooper, but he was just *such* a douchebag. I guess putting his dick in whatever skank he could find was his way of dealing with a broken heart.

"Lara?" he shouted again.

Placing my hands on my hips, I turned, the light breeze from cars driving by blew my blonde hair into my face. He shut off his bike and slid off his helmet, his hair drenched in sweat. He gave me a smile that made me shiver. *Damn him.* "What do you want, Luke?"

"I saw your car down the road and figured you needed help." He paused and raked his gaze down my body. "Unless you've got a new job I don't know about. You *are* looking pretty hot in those shorts."

I scoffed and muttered, "I guess I should've expected that, having a vagina and all."

He squinted and leaned forward. "What?"

"It was good of you to notice," I said loudly. "But I don't think many men will want me after I've been out here, sweating my ass off."

His gaze lowered to my hips. "We don't want that, now do we, cupcake? I like it the way it is. Where are you going?"

Rolling my eyes, I took a step back and continued

walking backward, refusing to give him another chance to check out my ass. "To the gas station. My car ran out of gas."

Grinning from ear to ear, he started his bike and slowly trailed me. "I see. Then it looks like I get to rescue you."

"More like patronize me. Why are you even here? Don't you have some groupies waiting for you somewhere?"

He chuckled and nodded toward something behind me. "Head's up."

Gasping, I turned around and almost walked headfirst into a road sign. I dodged it and turned right back around, giving him my front once again.

"I know my face is gorgeous and you can't get enough, but maybe you should turn around and watch where you're walking."

"As if." I huffed. "I don't want you staring at my ass. I know how you are."

"Then get on my bike. I'll take you to get some gas."

"No thanks. I'll do it on my own."

He revved his engine, his smile fading. "No, you're not, Lara. Now get on the damn bike." Turning around, he unhooked the extra helmet from the back and held it out to me. "It's a hundred degrees out here, you're being ridiculous."

I huffed and continued walking. "I'll be fine."

Slamming on the brakes, he got off his bike and stalked toward me. "You don't have any water, and I don't see anyone else stopping to give you a hand. Now stop being a silly woman, and get on the fucking bike."

"What, are you going to make me? Get over yourself. I'll be fine."

He cracked his knuckles. "I'll chase you down. You can't outrun me, cupcake. I wouldn't even try."

He was right, and it drove me crazy. I didn't want to be indebted to him under any circumstances, but would I really cut my nose off to spite my face? It was scorching out, and I didn't need to get heatstroke over this. "Fine, I'll come with you," I said, giving in.

A triumphant smile splayed across his face and I wanted to smack it off. He held the helmet out to me and I put it on, not having any idea how to work the straps.

Grabbing my waist, he pulled me toward him. "Here, let me fix it." His fingers brushed against my neck as he tightened the straps. After he was done, he stared at me with his sea-green eyes. "Feel okay?"

I nodded, though my patience was shot. "Peachy."

He got on his bike first and held out his hand. "Have you ever ridden before?"

"No." My stomach turned in knots.

He smirked. "You'll be okay, I promise. We don't have to go far. All you need to do is reach around my waist and hold on tight. It'll be over before you know it."

Taking my hand, he held it while I straddled his bike. It wasn't one of those big Harley ones either; it was a sleek, black sport bike. I reached around his waist to hold on, and my body was flush with his. After he put on his helmet, his hand landed on my thigh and my body tightened.

"You ready?"

"I think so."

He patted my leg and I sucked in a deep breath. *Here we go.*

Made in the USA
San Bernardino, CA
25 September 2016